'Captivating, serpentine and affecting ... It subverts the tropes of the "dead girl" genre in ways that impart its female characters with a dark majesty and mystery all their own' Megan Abbott

'Fascinating ... The book is less about the murder itself than about its aftermath, the long tendrils of guilt, sadness, anger and confusion that stretch out from a single act, wrapping themselves around everyone they touch' *New York Times Book Review*

'Nicola Maye Goldberg articulates a new kind of darkness within the female psyche – one that makes this book pulse forth with danger and suspense. Between the unexpected turns and the sharp sentences, it's nearly impossible to stop reading' Chelsea Hodson

'The writing here is sparkling and the detective work, refreshingly, internal rather than external ... Goldberg has a delightful eye for detail' *Observer*

'This unsettling, sinuous novel subtly explores the case's fallout among those closest to it' *Mail on Sunday*

'Tender, brutal, beautiful. This book haunts me' Kirsty Logan

'I can't think of another book with such unique story-telling ... So adept and intricate I devoured it in two sittings, then went back to revisit all the character links' Nina Pottell, *Prima*

NICOLA MAYE GOLDBERG is a graduate of Bard College and Columbia University. She is the author of *Other Women* and *The Doll Factory*. Her work has appeared in *CrimeReads*, the *Quietus, Queen Mob's Teahouse, Winter Tangerine*, and elsewhere. She lives in New York City.

nothing can hurt you

R A V E N BOOKS

LONDON · OXFORD · NEW YORK · NEW DELHI · SYDNEY

RAVEN BOOKS
Bloomsbury Publishing Plc
50 Bedford Square, London, WC1B 3DP, UK
29 Earlsfort Terrace, Dublin 2, Ireland

BLOOMSBURY, RAVEN BOOKS and the Raven Books logo
are trademarks of Bloomsbury Publishing Plc

First published in 2020 in the United States by Bloomsbury USA
First published in Great Britain by Raven Books 2020
This edition published 2021

A catalogue record for this book is available from the British Library

ISBN: HB: 978-1-5266-1944-0; TPB: 978-1-5266-1948-8;
PB: 978-1-5266-1947-1; eBook: 978-1-5266-1946-4

2 4 6 8 10 9 7 5 3 1

Typeset by Westchester Publishing Services
Printed and bound in Great Britain by CPI Group (UK) Ltd,
Croydon CR0 4YY

To find out more about our authors and books visit
www.bloomsbury.com and sign up for our newsletters

For my parents.

A soft light rising above the level meadow,
behind the bed. He takes her in his arms.
He wants to say *I love you, nothing can hurt you*

but he thinks
this is a lie, so he says in the end
you're dead, nothing can hurt you
which seems to him
a more promising beginning, more true.

—Louise Glück, "A Myth of Devotion"

Marianne

When I was six years old, my mother woke me at dawn and drove us to a motel in Morristown, New Jersey. I slept in the car and woke up in a dimly lit room that smelled of bleach and oranges. We stayed there almost two weeks, sleeping in the same bed, watching movies, and swimming in the pool, despite the thin layer of dead bugs and leaves that floated on the water.

At the time, my mother was going through a divorce, not from my father, but from a man named Dylan Novak. I don't remember being afraid of him, though maybe I should have been. My mom did a good job of making our time at the motel seem like a vacation, though she must have been out of her mind with fear.

Where Dylan is now, I don't know. Prison, maybe. Or dead, hopefully. Or scaring the shit out of some other woman. My father died when I was a baby. Sometimes I'm sure people know this just by looking at me, like they can sense that specific vulnerability. Even though I was too young to mourn him, fatherlessness shapes you.

In college I got into the occult—*The Golden Dawn*, Madame Blavatsky, conducting little séances in my dorm room. It's lucky that a cult never found me, because I would have been easy to recruit. My attempts to speak with ghosts disappointed me, probably because I was never really a believer. All the séances did was give me bad dreams. My father never appeared in those dreams, but Dylan did, laughing, rolling his eyes.

Shortly after I turned thirty, I began to have what my psychiatrists referred to as *episodes*. I hated that word, which made me think of sitcoms. Still, no one ever offered me a better one. It was hard to stand or to talk while they happened, and sometimes they lasted for hours. I didn't cry—crying would probably have been a relief. If I was in public, I dug my nails into my palms, leaving crescent moons in the flesh. Alone, I contorted my body into positions so strange I could never show them to anyone else, wrapping my limbs back around each other, like I was trying to become my own straitjacket.

At first it was just nausea. Then came images, as clear as if I were watching them on television. They were so violent. I saw myself stretched out on a piece of wood.

Then the wood snapped in half, and so did I, large splinters impaling me. I saw razor blades buried into my stomach so that only their silver handles were visible from the skin. I saw my skull crack open like an egg. They were not hallucinations, because I knew they were not real. Nor were they memories, or dreams, or things I'd seen in scary movies. It was like someone had gone inside my brain and left them there, like shards of glass across the floor. Needles.

These episodes are what drove us to move out of New York City, in the fall of 1997. At that point I had seen three therapists, two psychiatrists, an acupuncturist, a neurologist, a hypnotherapist, and a Reiki healer. Nothing and no one was helping. Also, it was getting harder to hide what was happening to me. My co-workers noticed that I left my desk to use the bathroom for hours at a time. My friends were uncertain about inviting me to dinners or parties because I might ruin it for everyone. My husband, whose kindness and generosity were superhuman, was almost as exhausted as I was.

So we moved upstate. It was my husband's idea. It was easy for him to find a job at a small bank in Rhinebeck. Though it was a step down from the one he had in the city, he said that because the cost of living was so much lower, it didn't matter.

He was sure that the fresh air and open space would be good for me. I agreed. We found a big yellow Victorian on the edge of a college town, with a backyard that extended into the woods, and beyond that, the river.

I had lots of ideas. I would get a dog, a big sweet one that would rest its head in my lap when I had an episode. I would grow vegetables in our backyard and cook with them. I would volunteer at the home for disabled children that was around the corner from us. I would learn about plant medicine. And at least I wouldn't have to grab on to a pillar when the train came by and I felt an overwhelming desire to jump in front of it.

"It's not good for humans to live in cities, Marianne," my husband told me. "We're not evolved for it. Today I saw a homeless man half-naked on the train, singing the national anthem. Staying here is taking years off our lives."

He was trying to make it seem like the move was for his benefit, as well, as if he weren't making an enormous sacrifice. This type of kindness was typical of him.

The drive up was so beautiful and peaceful. It was a clear day, just warm enough to drive with the windows down. First we listened to *Winterreise*, and then my husband turned the music off so we could enjoy the view properly, in half-reverent silence. All those enormous trees, the wide blue river—it was like we had wandered into a painting.

There were problems almost right away. The big one was that, having grown up in the city, I couldn't drive. I scheduled lessons, but I found it so difficult. It was amazing to me that so many people knew how to do it, as easily as walking, when it took up all my brainpower and then some. After each lesson I was exhausted and terrified. My face hurt from how tightly I clenched my jaw. And as the instructor helpfully reminded me, it would only get harder once there was ice on the road.

The second problem was the dog. We picked one out from a shelter, which made us feel virtuous. She was a tall, skinny animal that we thought might have been used for racing. I named her Shelley. She was very lazy, the shelter assured us, and affectionate, and would be happy to spend her days cuddling with me around the house. Shelley was nervous for the first few weeks we had her, which we knew was normal. I bought her a big soft bed and plenty of toys, and cooked her food myself—after all, I had time.

I really liked her. She had enormous dark eyes that absolutely melted me. When I took her for walks, the college students who lived near us fawned over her, telling me how much they missed their dogs at home, and she returned their affection with licks and wags.

But she hated my husband. The shelter had warned us that she was sometimes anxious around men, perhaps due to past abuse. *Just give her lots of time and space*, they instructed us, and that's what we did. The more Shelley liked me, the less she liked him. At first, she would hide under a chair when he entered a room. Then she started growling and baring her teeth when he came near me. One day she bit his hand so severely it required three stitches and a tetanus shot. He would have let me keep her, even after that, if I had asked, but I felt too guilty. We decided to wait a little while and try again.

The house was not what we had expected, either. It was beautiful and intricate on the outside, like a doll-house. But inside, the floors were uneven, the staircases absurdly steep, the plumbing unreliable at best. My husband assured me that this was just what big old houses were like, and I believed him. I scrubbed all the bathrooms with enough bleach to kill a person, but they still stank of mildew, which I realized was due to the old pipes. I got used to that.

I also got used to the way the doors opened and closed on their own if you left even one window open. The house had a big, beautiful backyard. I would look at it and think what a waste it was. For children or dogs, that backyard would have been heaven, but for us, it was just one more thing to maintain.

The episodes were not as frequent. They were happening only once or twice a week, instead of four or five times when we lived in the city. When they did occur, they were not quite as intense as before.

Also, I found a therapist I liked, in downtown Rhine-beck. I thought she might be a little kooky, because there were so many plants and crystals in her office, but I hoped they were just for decoration. I took a taxi to see her twice a week. Sometimes, if he could, my husband drove me. Sometimes we met for lunch after my appointments. I was even working a little, at a thrift store, not because we needed money, but to give my life a little structure. So we felt we had made the right choice, moving there.

Winter changed everything. We were unprepared. The house was freezing. We bought space heaters, but I was perpetually anxious that they would fall over and set the whole place on fire with us inside. My husband joked that we would just have to use our body heat, but that was not enough.

As it got colder, the roads got more dangerous, and the taxi service I used to get to my appointments became less and less reliable. My therapist was forgiving about me being late or missing them entirely, but it was still a problem. It also meant I spent much more time alone in that cold house, which seemed to me so spooky now that I didn't have a dog to protect and comfort me.

One day in early December my husband called me from work. He wanted to bring one of his friends to dinner that night, was that OK? I didn't feel like making conversation with a stranger, and our house was still full of cardboard boxes. But I could hardly say no. It's not like I had anything better to do than cook for three instead of two.

The friend, Ted Simpson, was a colleague from the bank, and he was distraught. He had missed as many days of work as he could get away with, and now when he came to the office, he was distracted and miserable. My husband tried to intervene on his behalf, to get him more sick days, but it didn't work.

His daughter, Meadow, from whom he had been estranged for many years, was missing. She had been in and out of rehabs and halfway houses since she was a teenager, but now she was really gone. Ted was tired from driving around all night, through the bad parts of Kingston and Poughkeepsie.

Meadow's mother had died when she was in kindergarten. I think my husband hoped that my fatherlessness and Meadow's motherlessness would create some kind of bond, and that I would be able to offer Ted some comfort. I could not. I could barely even cook him an edible meal.

As we ate, my husband and Ted discussed Meadow in low, solemn voices. My husband asked a lot of questions about her. He wanted to know how long Meadow had been gone, what the police were doing, if Ted thought it was enough. He asked if there was a reward for information. Maybe the bank could provide one. If not, maybe it could host some sort of fund-raiser. I thought Ted might be sick of answering questions like that, but he seemed grateful for the opportunity to talk about his daughter. I suspected most people in his life just didn't want to hear about anything so grim.

I admired how my husband was both practical and concerned. I wished that I could be more like him, but I was so cold and so tired. I kept seeing an image of myself with all my limbs fused together, like a rag doll sewn up wrong.

As they talked, I kept refilling their wineglasses. I sat with my sweetest, warmest facial expression, because I hoped that Ted would look over at me and see an image of comfort. My husband asked if I would help organize a fund-raiser, and I said yes, of course, I would be more than happy to. I was really doing my best. Ted left around midnight. My husband took a shower and fell asleep right away, because of all the wine. I stayed awake until dawn, staring at his kind, unconscious face.

Three weeks later, Ted came for dinner again. This time I ordered food from a restaurant, because I didn't want to subject such a sad man to my cooking. My husband and I had a small fight about that. He thought I was being lazy. *What are you doing all day that you can't even cook a decent meal?* he probably wanted to ask. When I explained it to him, he took me in his arms and kissed the top of my head.

"I doubt Ted has much of an appetite these days. The food is just a formality."

When Ted arrived, he was already a bit drunk. Who could blame him?

"I call the police every day. Local and state, to see if there are any updates. They talk to me like I'm some idiot. I want to yell, 'I pay your salaries! You work for me!' But

I can't afford to antagonize them," Ted told us. He was a big man, maybe fifty years old, who had lost the hair on top of his head, which made him look a bit like a clown. We sat in the kitchen because the big dining room was too cold. Ted kept his jacket on.

"It's a disgrace," my husband replied. He wanted to write letters and make phone calls. He was a man who believed that most things could be solved by letters and phone calls.

Ted occasionally tried to have a normal conversation with me about the house, if I missed the city. I replied politely and succinctly. I knew that he didn't really want to talk about any of that. Meadow had been gone for three months.

After dinner we switched from wine to whiskey. I wasn't supposed to drink hard liquor because of my medications, but my husband didn't say anything, and I sipped it carefully. It was clear that Ted was too drunk to drive home, so I set up a little bed for him in the room my husband sometimes used as an office. There was a big, comfortable couch downstairs, but I feared that the room would get too cold.

Around one in the morning my husband helped Ted upstairs. It was hard to tell in the half-light, but I thought that Ted might have been weeping.

"I hope you can get some rest," my husband said. "Good night."

The idea of a grown man sleeping on our squeaky, flimsy futon, in a room still full of unpacked boxes, made me so sad. I went downstairs to see if I could find any extra blankets or pillows to make him more comfortable. There was one wool throw, a wedding present, that we sometimes used when we watched television. I decided to take it up to him.

I knocked on the door.

"Come in," said Ted.

He was sitting on the edge of the futon. His shoes were off, but he was still fully dressed. I could have just handed him the blanket, but instead I draped it around his shoulders. As I did, he pulled me toward him and stuck his cold hand up my skirt.

He was a tired, drunk old man, and I could have stopped him with a slap, but I didn't. I looked around the room, like I hoped for someone who could tell me, *Yes, this is really happening*. But, of course, it was just the two of us.

He squeezed me so hard. I later thought it must have been the pain, more than anything else, that interested him. I just stood there. Part of me felt sorry for him, and part of me felt scared. Neither part of me could move. After what felt like a long time, he removed his hand and turned away from me.

I went to take a shower. My husband was already asleep. What upset me the most, I realized, was not the pain but Ted's certainty that I would not scream. He was that sure of my pity and shame. As I crawled into bed in the darkness, I was terrified of what my brain would show me. But there was only emptiness.

The snow had fallen so heavily overnight that Ted could not get his car out of our driveway. He and my husband spent all day watching TV, playing Risk, and drinking whiskey. They ate leftovers. I pretended to be busy in bed with a book, when I was really sitting with the emptiness. For the first time I longed for one of my visions. I wanted to see Ted's head crack open, to see myself scooping out his brain with my fingernails. It took two days for the snow to melt. Ted suggested calling a tow truck, but when my husband said that he was free to stay with us, to get some rest, he happily agreed.

On the third day, I made breakfast, a really good breakfast, home fries and bacon and eggs and tomatoes. We all sat around eating and talking and reading the newspaper. When my husband got up to use the bathroom, I leaned over and whispered in Ted's ear.

"Your daughter is dead. Everybody knows it. She was raped and killed and left in an alley like garbage."

Then I cleared my plate and went upstairs.

About an hour later, my husband came into our room without knocking.

"Marianne, what is wrong with you?" he asked. The question was not rhetorical. I was silent.

"What kind of a person says something like that?" He seemed on the verge of tears even as he towered over me.

I could not respond. I could not tell him what Ted had done to me, even though it might make him forgive me. But when I looked at his face, I did not see even a scrap of love or affection. He was looking at me like he was trying to figure out exactly how badly he'd fucked up his life for my sake, and how he was going to fix it. He looked like he wanted me dead.

"I'm going for a walk" was all I said. I put on my boots and a coat that was not nearly warm enough and went into the woods. The melting snow made it muddy, but it was still beautiful, a clean blanket placed over the world. *So this is why people live up here*, I thought.

When I got to the river, I saw a girl, her flesh all white and blue, half-covered in dirt and leaves. I knew immediately that she was dead, but I wasn't sure if she was real or not. I knelt beside her and took off my glove to touch her face. Then I ran back to my house to call the police.

When I got there, both my husband's and Ted's cars were gone. The heat was off. I was shaking so badly it was hard to dial the numbers. By the time the police arrived—two men in uniform—I had not calmed down. Speaking felt as painful and unnatural as pulling out my own teeth. They asked if I could lead them to the body. I said I would try. As they followed me through the woods, I wondered if they thought I was insane. When we reached her, I felt a twinge of triumph. Then I vomited all over one of the officers.

It wasn't until weeks later, when I was living with my mother, that I learned who it was. She was a college girl named Sara who had been killed by her boyfriend. I was afraid that I would be called to testify, that I would have to tell them how I found her.

If I had, I might have told them: What I felt when I saw that frozen face was not fear or disgust. It was relief. It lasted only a moment, but it was so profound that it bordered on joy.

Katherine

T here were parts of Florida that really did look like heaven—Katherine had seen them on the drive from the airport. Paradise Lake Recovery Center looked more like Eden, after God and Man and the more discerning animals had deserted it. The whole property was overgrown with banyan trees—which were also known as strangler trees, according to her cabinmate Rachelle. Katherine found this both appropriate and disturbing. Though the staff tried to maintain suburban-style lawns around each of the cabins and the main buildings, the grass was always patchy and muddy, with strange weeds growing defiantly around the edges.

Paradise Lake's website had promised a "camp-like" atmosphere, which Katherine did not consider very appealing. She had always hated summer camp. There were six female and five male cabins, each with four residents at a time. Katherine had never been inside the male cabins, as per the strict guidelines, but she doubted that they looked much different. Vaguely rustic, but mercifully clean, with white walls and Ikea furniture. Her cabin included framed paintings of the ocean and decorative pillows embroidered with the serenity prayer. LIVE LAUGH LOVE! commanded a wrought-iron wall decal. Katherine was not the violent type, but she was a little surprised that no one else had ever tried to bludgeon someone with it, considering that it was attached to the wall with nothing but a flimsy hook. It remained there during her entire four-month stay. Even with the lights off, she could still see its vague outline, taunting her.

When she arrived, Katherine was twenty-eight, which was young for an alcoholic. *I'm practically a prodigy*, she told her parents over the phone. They didn't laugh. Katherine hated that she came from such humorless people. When she repeated the same line to Blake, he called her the Mozart of Substance Abuse.

If she'd met Blake at a party, or a bar, Katherine would have liked him a lot. It helped that he was movie-star handsome, the kind of handsome that shifted the air in the room when he walked in. Because she met him in rehab, where they weren't allowed to touch, she loved him right away.

It was weird, the people you ended up liking at a place like that. One of Katherine's favorites was a fat, red-haired former frat boy named Jimmy, who was in rehab instead of prison after getting drunk and killing a woman with his car. He was from a wealthy family, and the sentencing had caused a huge outrage in the Georgia town where it happened. There was even a petition to oust the judge in the case. Under different circumstances, Katherine probably would have signed it. Of course Jimmy deserved to go to jail. But he was friendly, and told great jokes at the expense of the therapists, and so Katherine was glad he hadn't.

"You are not a good person." That's one of the first things Katherine's primary therapist, Arthur, had told her. "Once you get over that, you might figure out how to be functional."

Arthur was sixty years old, but looked older. He looked like he had died of old age and been resurrected for the sole purpose of yelling at addicts. Of everyone at Paradise Lake, Katherine hated him the most, despite plenty of competition. He was a dickhead, and he made her cry during almost every session. He talked to her like she was the worst person in the world, like she had drowned babies in a bathtub or set a nursing home on fire.

She preferred Lucy, who ran her morning group, and who started and ended each meeting with a prayer, even though Paradise Lake was technically a secular treatment center. Lucy had frizzy hair and huge eyes that made her look like she had recently been electrocuted. She rarely gave advice, just listened intently, and occasionally shushed a person who was interrupting someone else's story. Katherine always left morning group a bit calmer than before, ready to make a collage or go for a nature walk or whatever other preschool-level activity would be required of her that day.

Arthur, however, was known for getting results. At least two former residents had named kids after him. Katherine imagined little Arthurs running around all over the country, shoelaces untied, screaming motivational quotes on the playground.

Some of the people at Paradise Lake were sort of glamorous. There was even a famous country singer, but she left a couple of days after Katherine arrived. One girl around Katherine's age was an heiress who as a child watched her father kill her mother. He smashed the mother's head in with the claw end of a hammer. *Daddy painted her red*, she told the police. Her name was Carmen, and she was exactly as fucked up as Katherine would have expected, but she was also kind of a bitch, always muttering mean things under her breath during group and refusing to share her cigarettes.

Blake was, relatively speaking, pretty similar to Katherine. He had also grown up in suburbia—she in Oregon, he in Maine. He liked to read, and they traded books sometimes. He lent her books by Dostoyevsky and Céline and many other authors Katherine had pretended to read in college. In return, she lent him a biography of Marie-Antoinette, which she enjoyed even though it gave her weird dreams about having her head cut off.

He called her Katie, which she found endearing. Even as a kid, she'd always been a Katherine, sometimes a Kat. He must have thought that it suited her.

Once, when he found her crying after an exhausting session with Arthur, he told her: "If I looked like you, I'd never be sad."

It was the strangest and the best compliment she'd ever received. Katherine knew that she was not beautiful, though she suspected she had been, once. Now her face was bloated and scarred from acne, and the Florida sun had bleached her hair in a way she felt made her resemble a pumpkin. For a second she wondered if Blake was making fun of her. But the way he kept his pale gaze fixed on her suggested otherwise.

His eyes were an intense blue. *Cracked out*, Rachelle called them, but Katherine liked them. She had never seen a boy with eyes that pretty.

Everyone gossiped at Paradise Lake, because despite the swimming pool and the tennis court and the infinite supply of arts and crafts, there was really nothing better to do. That's how Katherine found out that Blake had murdered someone.

Carmen told her, a week before Katherine left. She must have let it slip somehow that she liked Blake—by looking at him too much, or laughing at one of his jokes, and Carmen noticed.

"Don't you know what he did?" she asked Katherine, as they stood in line for dessert, which was brownie bites, unnecessarily arranged in the shape of a heart.

"Nope," said Katherine, not looking at Carmen, not wanting to give her the satisfaction.

"Do you want to know? Maybe you don't. It's pretty bad."

"Either tell me or don't tell me."

"He killed his girlfriend. He took her into the woods and slit her throat," Carmen said, miming the action, just in case Katherine didn't get it. Carmen still had rich-girl hair, which fell in soft gold waves across her shoulders, but her teeth were rotten. "Just fucking left her there to die. Took them two days to find her."

Katherine had a million questions. Internet access was strictly forbidden at Paradise Lake, which meant she was going to have to rely on Carmen for answers.

"Two days?" she said, stupidly, as if that were the most interesting part of the information.

"Yup." Carmen frowned. She had probably been expecting a more extreme reaction.

"That's fucked up," Katherine said, evenly.

"Yup. It really is. Do you have any cigarettes?"

. . .

Paradise Lake's official motto was A Place for Healing. Its real motto was *Hurt people hurt people*. Katherine wondered where the hurt came from in the first place. She imagined it pooled at the center of the earth, like oil.

During yoga, Katherine decided to find out if Jimmy, who shared a cabin with Blake, knew anything.

"Do you know why he's here?" she asked, as they did downward dog.

"Depression, he said," answered Jimmy. He turned his face, red with effort, toward her. "Why do you ask?"

"Just curious. Carmen said he killed someone."

"Really? No shit." Jimmy seemed a little impressed.

"She could be making it up."

"Carmen does love lying," Jimmy acknowledged. "But it would kind of make sense. Maybe he did that, felt super guilty, so he tried to off himself, and now he's here."

You would know about feeling super guilty, Katherine was tempted to say. But instead she exhaled and moved into cat pose.

The worst part of rehab, next to all the rules, was that people said stupid shit all the time, and you weren't allowed to make fun of them. It made her worry that she herself was going to start saying stupid shit, and wouldn't even realize it, because no one would tell her. It was nerve-racking. In evening group, a middle-aged former crackhead named Billy said, in total seriousness, "I'm interested in interesting things. Like neuroscience, and how the moon looks like a face."

Everyone had nodded and murmured their assent, and Katherine wanted to scream. She had been there for five months, and she had three days left.

After group, she declined Lucy's invitation to arts and crafts hour, and instead walked to the pool. No one ever swam in it, because no one ever cleaned it, because there was no need to, because no one ever swam in it. It was a ten-by-twenty-foot representation of human folly, coated in algae.

Katherine hitched up her skirt and stuck her feet in the water. It was gross, but it still felt good. She sat there for a while, smoking cigarette after cigarette, staring at the stars, trying not to despair.

"Hello," said Blake, startling her.

"Hi." Katherine glanced around. It was rare for male clients and female clients to be left alone together, even in a setting as profoundly unsexy as this one. Usually a staff member would intervene. Maybe everyone was busy. Or maybe, because Katherine was leaving so soon, they had given up on her. They had to prioritize, after all. Blake sat down next to her, cross-legged.

"I had a dream about you, Katie. You had wings. But they were bird-sized. Like, small. In the middle of your back. You couldn't fly but you kept showing them off."

Katherine felt a shiver of pleasure down her back, right in the location of her dream-wings. She swirled her feet around in the water, examining the ripples.

"What color were they?"

"Green."

"Like a parrot's?"

"I guess."

"That's good. Could be gross little gray pigeon wings."

Thanks to the new cocktail of medications from her Paradise Lake psychiatrists, Katherine no longer remembered her dreams, which she was glad of, because if she did, she would have to tell Arthur about them. Those doctors knew what they were doing, even if you did have to wonder how they ended up in the middle of Florida, ministering to junkies.

She watched Blake take off his shoes and roll up the hems of his jeans, and felt another shiver. It had been three months since she'd been touched by anyone, except to shake hands with Arthur at the beginning of each session. It wasn't natural, she thought. It was enough to drive a person crazy, even under the best of circumstances. When she was out of there, she would write Paradise Lake a letter, telling them so.

"Did you ever try that?" he asked, gesturing to the crowd of people on horses in the distance.

"Equine therapy?"

"No, escaping on horseback."

Katherine laughed. "No. I don't like horses. They're huge, and they smell like their own shit."

"True," he said. "Good thing that they're vegetarians, right?"

"What?"

"Like, if they ate meat? That would be really scary."

"Oh shit. I never even thought of that! Shit. That's fucked up."

They both laughed.

"Did you really kill your girlfriend?" she asked, trying to use a light, flirtatious tone of voice, but she was out of practice. It came out silly, high-pitched, and she cringed at the sound of it.

"Yes," he said.

"Really?"

"Really. I was on acid. I had some kind of a psychotic episode. It was like I was someone else, watching someone do this terrible thing. I closed my eyes, so that I wouldn't have to see it. And then when I opened them again, I was in a jail cell."

He did not seem angry, or even offended, which is what Katherine had expected. He didn't sound particularly remorseful, either.

"What was she like?"

"Lovely. Very clever, very sweet. She was a brilliant painter. You would have liked her. Everyone did." He said this without any discernible emotion, not meeting

Katherine's gaze. She shifted, trying to keep her face still. After all, how was one supposed to talk about a girl they'd stabbed to death?

"Do you miss her?"

"Every second of every day." That, at least, sounded sincere.

"Is that why they made you come here? Because you killed someone?"

"No. No one made me come here. It was my idea. I've been depressed, very horribly depressed, for a long time. I thought they might be able to help me here."

So Jimmy had been partly correct.

"Why didn't you go to prison?"

"I was found not guilty by reason of temporary insanity." He gave a short, hollow laugh. "Not to brag or anything, but it's pretty rare, that verdict. It's just, like, me and that lady who cut off her husband's dick."

Katherine winced. "How did you get it, then?"

"Well, I had a pretty good lawyer, and no criminal history. I think the judge could tell, you know, that I really loved her. That I never would have done something like that to her if I was in my right mind. And well, you know, it probably helped a lot that I'm white."

Oh great, thought Katherine. *A racially sensitive murderer.*

"I was in a mental hospital for two months. Jesus, if you think you meet some weirdos here . . ."

He grinned, the kind of grin Katherine had always been a sucker for, both broad and apologetic, revealing a single dimple on the left side of his face.

"Wow," she said. She moved her feet in circles around the dirty water, not looking at him.

"Why did you have a knife with you?" she asked, finally. "Where did you get it?"

"The knife?" He seemed confused for a moment. "Oh. It belonged to my friend Sam. He was into outdoorsy stuff, hiking, all that. It was a survival knife."

"That's kind of ironic," Katherine said.

His face darkened. He looked more sad than angry, and Katherine was so embarrassed that in her haste to change the subject, she didn't realize that he hadn't really answered her question.

He continued. "When I got out of the hospital, I moved back home. None of my old friends wanted anything to do with me. Which I understand. Even my family was nervous around me. I had dreams about Sara all the time. Nightmares, really. It got to a point where I could barely tell when I was sleeping and when I was awake, because I was so fucking tired. And I couldn't talk to anyone about it."

Katherine nodded. However weird and incomprehensible the rest of his story was to her, she knew what it was like to be that lonely.

"I'm an alcoholic," she said, even though he probably already knew that. "I was a party girl in college. I had lots of friends. We had so much fun. But then everyone else grew up and moved on, and I didn't."

She felt stupid after she said it—why was she trying to convince him they had something in common? But he nodded, and said, kindly: "It's hard, feeling alone."

"Is being here good for you? Does it help?"

"Yes. I like the routine. I like talking to people. I like talking to you."

"Before I came here, I got so drunk, I almost died. In the hospital, I stopped breathing twice." She paused. "I was legally dead." Actually, she was uncertain of the precise legal parameters of death, but she was pretty sure that she was telling the truth. "But that's not why I came here. I came here because my parents said they would stop sending me money if I didn't. I was more scared of not having money than I was of being dead."

He nodded, slowly. "That makes sense, actually. Often death is too abstract for people to process fully. Especially young people. Money is just more real."

He was right, of course. She felt a small lift inside her chest, like a window opening, cool air rushing in.

Years ago, while she was taking time off from college, Katherine worked at a bookstore in her hometown. One day, a woman came in to purchase books for someone in prison. The whole process was complicated, but being the nice liberals that they were, Katherine and her co-worker helped the woman sort it out. The books she chose were *The Stone Diaries* and *Amsterdam*. Later Katherine's co-worker looked up the name of the recipient and discovered that he was serving ten years for the rape of a thirteen-year-old girl. "Well, at least she didn't send him *Lolita*," said Katherine, a little too blithely. *Doing a bad thing doesn't make you a bad person*, Lucy had said, more than once. It was comforting, but at some point, it must cease to be true. There must be a certain threshold of bad things that did in fact reflect on your character. It's just that no one was really qualified to make that call.

And what about forgiveness? Certain things had to be unforgivable, otherwise the whole concept was meaningless.

So Katherine had never cut anyone's throat or run them over with a car. She was still selfish, impulsive, destructive, an embarrassment to her family, a toddler inside the body of a grown woman. *There's more than enough time for redemption*, Arthur told her, more than once. *That's why you're so lucky you got here while you're still young.*

So, what, should she spend the rest of her life volunteering in fucking soup kitchens?

"Well," Arthur replied, "I was thinking more along the lines of, getting a fucking job."

A job. Something benign, maybe at a library. Or a vet's office. She'd always loved animals, and maybe she could get used to the smell. A job, AA meetings, a shitty little apartment with plants on the windowsill, new friends, a cat, perhaps, dinner with her parents every week, grocery shopping, laundry, falling asleep in front of the television.

One day at a time, that's what addicts were supposed to live by, and Katherine had to admit there was a certain appeal to that. Who couldn't make it through one day at a time? But days turn into weeks, into years, into lifetimes, and then one day you were dead, with nothing to show for yourself except maybe you hadn't fucking killed anybody.

She forgave Blake, but it was irrelevant. She didn't forgive him because he deserved it, but because she loved him, and she probably only loved him because he was handsome and kind to her and also because they were stuck in this muggy self-righteous hellhole together. However much joy he brought her, it could not possibly equal the sorrow he brought to others. *It's not that precise of an equation*, Arthur might say. But it was still one worth considering.

Katherine left Paradise Lake and moved back to Oregon, to her parents' house. She and her dad put a cot and a small desk in the attic so that she could have a little privacy while living with them. They also painted the walls white, with a blue trim. It reminded her, not unpleasantly, of a baby's bedroom.

She got a job at a shoe store. To her surprise, she liked working there. She liked making small talk with customers, smiling at them, giving them compliments. The constant facade of happiness actually made her a little happier. Arthur would probably have something to say about that. Twice a week, she went to an AA meeting. Sometimes she took the bus, and sometimes one of her parents drove her.

The very first day her parents left her in the house alone, she went online to look for information about the girl Blake killed. There was almost nothing. Did college boys just murder their girlfriends so often that it was no longer newsworthy? It took her twenty minutes to find an article from the *Dutchess County Weekly*. It was headlined COLLEGE SLASHER FOUND INSANE. The article itself was behind a paywall. Katherine tried to sign up for a free trial period, but the website required a credit card. She didn't have a credit card. Her parents had confiscated her debit card two years ago, and they kept their credit cards in a safe or on their persons at all times.

She had to wait until her sister, Eleanor, came to visit. Eleanor, her husband, and their five-year-old son, Jackson, slept in Katherine's room, and Katherine set up a blow-up bed in the office. During the day she played with Jackson, who was mainly interested in the many issues of *National Geographic Kids* he had brought with him. Katherine sat with him on her lap in the living room and read page after page of facts about zoo animals.

When it was nighttime and everyone was asleep, Katherine walked, soft-footed, into her room, where her sister's handbag was hanging from the closet door. She slipped the wallet out without a sound. Safely in the office, she left the cash where it was and used her sister's credit card to subscribe to the newspaper.

Despite its horror movie title, the article was disappointing. It confirmed what Carmen had said, that Blake killed his girlfriend in the woods with a knife. "There's no happy ending here," one of the prosecutors said. "In this case, the guilt Mr. Campbell will live with for the rest of his life is more than enough punishment." Blake's lawyer was quoted, too, calling the murder "a tragedy." The article said that Blake had sobbed in court and apologized to his dead girlfriend's family. Katherine wondered how they reacted to that, how they felt. It was, of course, impossible to imagine. They must have been furious to see him go free. Unless they believed that he really didn't mean to do it, that it was a tragedy and not a crime. Which was easier to live with?

As she lay in her blow-up bed, Katherine thought of Blake. She missed him. She wanted to tell him all the boring details of her life, and for him to say strange things about them. It was shocking how much she missed him. It reminded her of the summer camp she'd hated as a child, of how homesick she was. She felt as awful and as lonely as she had back then, sitting on the top bunk, writing letters to her parents, begging for them to come and take her home.

She remembered a magazine article she'd read, about the women who wrote letters to Charles Manson in prison, who proposed marriage. Women so sad, it was disgusting. But Blake wasn't like Manson. He'd only killed one person, and it wasn't even on purpose, not really. It occurred to her that maybe the difference between a killer and a murderer is whether you're allowed to forgive them.

This wasn't a conversation she wanted to have with herself. She just wanted to see Blake's eyes, and if she couldn't do that, to tell him that she was having dreams again, silvery things that meant nothing but were a relief anyhow, a sign that her brain would belong to her again soon.

Katherine took her mother's cell phone from its charger in the kitchen and slipped into the backyard. She found Paradise Lake's number saved in the contacts. A voice she didn't recognize answered.

"Hello, this is Paradise Lake, a place to heal. How may I direct your call?"

"Uh, hi. It's me, Katherine. I want to speak to Blake, if he's still awake?"

"I'm sorry," said the voice. "I can't confirm or deny that he's here. But I can take a message."

"No, it's OK," she said, stupidly. "I'm a former resident. He's my friend."

"I can't confirm or deny that he's here," the voice said, again. "But I can take a message."

"Why would you take a message for someone who isn't even there?" Katherine asked, irritably.

"That's our policy, miss. I'm sorry." The voice didn't sound apologetic at all. Katherine sighed loudly.

"OK. Uh, tell him Katherine called. And happy Thanksgiving."

"Would you like to leave your number?"

"Um, sure."

Katherine hung up the phone, exhausted. No wonder none of her friends had ever called her. All that stupidity probably scared them off.

"The moment you say, this pain is unendurable, you are already enduring," Arthur had said. But this wasn't pain. It was something silkier and stranger than that. She sat down on the grass and wrapped her arms around her knees, making herself very small.

Juliet

I met Celeste Hamilton while we were covering the trial of John Logan, the Kingston Killer. She was reporting on the trial for a well-regarded magazine based in New York City. I was covering it for a small local newspaper. I envied Celeste's job, if not her commute. I had read some of her articles before and recognized her from her author picture: elegant cheekbones, a white-blonde bob. I thought it was admirable that she was pretty enough for television but worked in print anyway.

Celeste was the one who nicknamed Logan the Kingston Killer, even though he technically lived in Barrytown. The alliteration didn't do what it was supposed to, which was catch the public's imagination. No one seemed to care that much about John Logan, because no one cared that much about the women he killed.

As far as serial killers go, Logan was boring. No genius-level IQ, no cryptic messages to the police, no delusions of grandeur. He simply killed six women and buried them in the backyard of his house. In his mug shot, his eyes were as pale as a blind man's, his face waxy and drawn.

"It's too bad he never ate anyone's hands, or anything," Celeste said to me, the first time we spoke. "That could have made your career."

I laughed in shock because, of course, she was right. At first, I hoped that she would be a kind of mentor, but as time went on, we were both too exhausted for that. "I just don't have the stomach for this kind of thing anymore," she confessed to me, less than a week into the trial. "This fucked-up shit. Maybe it's because I had kids. They made me soft."

I did not have the excuse of motherhood. I worried that I was just weak.

That winter, I was also working on an article about a Crawford College student named Sara Morgan, who had been murdered by her boyfriend a month after Logan was arrested. Her body was found by a local housewife in the woods that surrounded Crawford College—only twelve miles from Kingston. Sara's boyfriend, a diagnosed schizophrenic who had recently graduated from Crawford, had confessed almost immediately.

I told Celeste about this while she stirred her milkshake with a long metal spoon.

"It's creepy," she said. "But there's not a connection, is there?"

"Not literally," I admitted. "But I think, maybe, in a larger sense——"

Celeste cut me off. "I know the article you're thinking of writing, and they are almost never any good." She paused. "Maybe yours will be."

It wasn't the kind of encouragement I was hoping for, but it was unfair to expect much enthusiasm from Celeste about anything at that point. Neither one of us was sleeping well. A few times a week, I got stomachaches so painful that I couldn't sit up straight.

But I kept researching Sara Morgan's case, long after I had to, for reasons I couldn't fully articulate to myself. I felt bad about it, like it meant I didn't care enough about Logan's victims. Maybe I was bored with them. Celeste was right. There was no real connection.

Even if Logan hadn't been in jail when Sara died, he still wouldn't have been a suspect. He strangled his victims. Sara Morgan's throat was cut so deeply, according to the coroner, that her vertebrae were exposed.

My articles were usually human interest, cutesy things: local firehouse dog honored, controversy over parking kiosk, high school auditorium dedicated to late teacher.

Bad things happened here, like they happened everywhere—local man dead of a drug overdose, local woman indicted for vehicular manslaughter—but they were not my department. Our regular crime reporter was on maternity leave, so the Logan trial became my responsibility.

My newspaper had written about Sara Morgan three times. The first headline was SEARCH INTENSIFIES FOR CRAWFORD STUDENT. We covered her again when her body was found and her boyfriend charged with murder, and a third time when he was found not guilty by reason of temporary insanity. There was no need, according to my editor, for an update. The case was as closed as a case could be.

That didn't deter me from driving to the Crawford campus to see if anyone would talk to me. This was during the third month of Logan's trial.

The students at Crawford were mostly dressed in dark wool coats and leather shoes. There were none of the crazy dyed hair and arms full of bracelets that I remembered from my own college days.

I found a girl drinking coffee by herself inside the campus center. Her dark lipstick had stained the edge of the paper cup. She told me her name was Odile. I introduced myself as a reporter, and her eyebrows shot up. When I named the paper, she looked a little disappointed.

"I'm writing an article about Sara Morgan," I lied. "Did you know her?"

"Oh, no. I mean, it's a small school, so everyone kind of knows everyone. But we weren't, like, friends."

"What about her boyfriend?"

"No. I've seen him around. He's really handsome." She shook her head apologetically. "That's weird to say. Sorry. I've never spoken to him."

"OK." I made my voice gentle. "Can you tell me how you heard about the murder?"

She flinched at the word. Beneath her heavy makeup, she looked extremely young. I wondered if she'd skipped a grade or two at some point.

"They had an assembly. The president made an announcement. It was terrible. People were screaming and crying. I was crying, too, and I didn't even know her. It's just awful."

"People were upset?"

"Well, yeah."

"I'm just curious about the atmosphere on campus. How people have reacted. What they're saying." All these college kids, most of them from respected, white, upper-middle-class families. This was probably the closest to violence they had ever been.

"It's . . . weird. I don't know. People are sad, but it's not like we're the most cheerful bunch of people to begin with, you know? I think we're starting to get back to normal."

Sara Morgan had died only three months earlier. To a bunch of eighteen-year-olds, I supposed, that might as well be an eternity. I thanked the girl for her time and left her my card.

I told Celeste about my trip, hoping she would admire my determination. She didn't.

"It sounds like a depressing waste of time," she said. "Don't you have enough death to deal with?"

"I could ask you the same thing. You've been covering this shit for years." I almost said decades, but I didn't want her to think that I thought she was old.

She shook her head. "I've built up my immunity. You have to do it slowly. Otherwise you'll have a nervous breakdown. You might have one anyway."

What did she mean, her immunity? Hadn't she just told me how having kids had weakened her? I was beginning to suspect that Celeste's advice, though given with absolute confidence, was at least partly bullshit. I slurped my milkshake, feeling despondent.

"The NGRI is interesting," Celeste admitted. "Those are rare. Even for rich kids."

"I know," I said.

"He must have had a good lawyer. Someone expensive. That could be your angle."

"Maybe," I said. I didn't want to tell her that I didn't really give a shit about the boyfriend. Sara was the one I wanted to write about.

"Look at this," Celeste said, gesturing around the diner, which was empty except for us and an old woman delicately eating a salad. "Six dead women. It should be a media circus. But no one gives a shit." We were now three months into the trial, and the only reporters who still showed up every day. Sometimes Celeste slept on my couch when she was too tired to drive back to the city.

"Maybe Sara Morgan would make them give a shit," I said.

She shook her head, a little annoyed. "Do you know how many college girls get killed by their shitty boyfriends?"

I didn't answer.

"It's a rhetorical question," she admitted, slurping. "I don't have the exact statistics. But, a lot."

I considered asking about her daughter. I knew that she had one, though she rarely spoke about her. Given what Celeste saw every day, how did she resist the temptation to lock her daughter in a tower? I wanted to lock myself in a tower most of the time. Maybe being a parent required a kind of willful stupidity, a belief that your child would neither be the person to whom something terrible happened nor be the person who did the terrible thing. I wished I could ask her, but in the context of what we were discussing, the topic felt obscene.

I moved to upstate New York after graduate school because my boyfriend, Sean, had inherited a house from his mother. I could never get used to that part of the world, how unrelentingly grim it was, with its empty houses, its disused gas stations and naked trees lining the highway. Winter was actually a relief, the snow covering everything like a thick, soft blanket.

According to Sean, it was not always like that. A lot of people moved up to Poughkeepsie to work at IBM in the early 1980s, including his father. It was, briefly, a nice place to live. In 1993 the company cut over three thousand jobs, and the area has been suffering ever since.

When we first moved here, Sean took me to a restaurant in downtown Saugerties. As we were ordering appetizers, a woman came up and started licking the window, her whole tongue, dotted with sores, pressed flat against the glass.

At home, I hung up my coat and sat down at my desk with a glass of whiskey. Next to my computer was a bright purple sticky note with the names and ages of all of Logan's victims.

Jasmine Ware, 32
Paulina Gonzales, 31
Meadow Simpson, 24
Mary Knapp, 27
Amber Lawson, 33
Vanessa Freeman, 19

Sara Morgan was twenty-one years old. I wished that I had chosen a different color. The purple struck me now as garish, maybe even disrespectful.

I decided to call my mother. She lived in the city. I spoke to her two or three times a week on the telephone, and visited at least once a month.

"Hi, Mom. Everything OK?"

My mother was a psychiatrist. Her office, on the Upper West Side of Manhattan, was decorated with white orchids in terra-cotta bowls, and blue douppioni curtains. Framed above her desk was a drawing I made when I was five or six, of a golden retriever wearing a crown. I wasn't sure how I came up with that. We never had a dog. My dad was allergic.

"Yes. How are you?"

"I'm good. I'm a little worn-out. This trial . . ." I didn't really want to talk to her about it.

"Oh, I'm sure. Is it almost done?"

"Hard to know."

"Those poor girls," she said, and I knew that she was saying that because she didn't know anything about them yet. Not that my mother would say that they deserved to die for being poor or trashy or unlucky, but she, like many, would prefer to save her grief for the Sara Morgans of the world. It is snobbishness, and a particularly cruel variety of it, but it's something else as well. At a certain point, you realize the world is so bad, that it's easier to pretend that people deserve the terrible things that befall them. That way, at least, you can pretend that you are safe.

"Are you proud of it?" she asked me.

"What?"

"Of what you're writing, Juliet. Do you think it's good work?"

If I were a teacher, I would give myself a B. If I was generous.

"Yes."

"And it's not—you know. Those awful trashy pieces that they always write about these sorts of things."

People write awful trash because other people read it, is what I wanted to say. She was right that sometimes stories about violence were gratuitous and exploitative. But sometimes they were just true.

"No. Just the facts. Nothing lurid."

"Good, good. You know, I was thinking, maybe you should come to the city for your birthday. We can do something nice. Go for dinner."

My thirty-third birthday. Thirty-three, with no husband, no children, and a career not nearly glittering enough to justify those absences.

"Oh. That's really nice of you. Sean and I already have plans, though."

"Of course. Just thought I'd ask." She sounded a little skeptical. We both knew that Sean wasn't a plan-making kind of person, though he did, occasionally, come through.

"I should get going," I told her. "Still have work to do."

"Of course. I love you."

"I love you, too."

The click of the line warmed me with relief.

I wondered about the parents of Sara's killer. His father ran a small but successful chain of health food stores in New Hampshire and Maine. His mother taught middle school French. He had an older sister, Gemma, who was also present at his hearing. She had her first child in June.

Being a parent sounded like hell to me. Mr. and Mrs. Campbell probably spent at least two decades dealing with the terror of their daughter ending up like Sara (or

Meadow, or Jasmine). What would they do now that their own son was one of those people they've been afraid of all these years?

Once, when I was in high school, I stole four tubes of cheap lipstick from a drugstore—two pink, one red, one purple. When my mother found them, price tags still stuck on, under the sink in the bathroom, she told me that the next time I did something like that, she'd call the police herself. *I wouldn't be a good parent if I protected you from the consequences of your own actions*, she said.

The killer's parents had hired a lawyer, a good one, from New York, to represent their son. Did that make them bad parents? Bad people? He and Sara had dated for almost three years. Surely Sara had met his family, maybe even visited them once or twice. Did they spend the holidays together? Had she ever joined them on a family vacation? Did she send Gemma a baby present? Were they invited to Sara's funeral? When I spoke to them, all they would say was that they were very sad for the Morgans' loss. Their son's lawyer, I suspected, had instructed them not to say anything else.

I finished my whiskey and poured myself another glass, then drank it as I stared out at the snow and waited, anxiously, for Sean to come home.

The feeling wasn't new—I had felt it, in varying levels of intensity, since I met him—but it got worse after I started covering the Logan case. I wasn't completely sure why. It was a kind of horror that made me crave intimacy. It made me crave this man, who was, statistically, the person most likely to murder me. Sean and I met at a party during my second year of graduate school. We slept together that night, at his house, on his dirty bed with its dark blue sheets.

A week later, I ran into him at the grocery store. He hugged me and kissed my cheek. He greeted me with such joy, as if I were a childhood friend, as if I were someone he had loved for a long time, not a girl he'd fucked once. I really liked that. I gave him my number, and he called me the next day.

Four days a week, Sean works at a retirement home. The rest of his time he dedicates to playing keyboards in his band, Kill Olivia.

"Who is Olivia?" I asked him once.

"Uh, no idea. They were called that before I joined."

"You never asked?"

"No. I don't think it's even a real person, honestly. It just sounds good."

I stood in the kitchen for a long time, staring out the window. Then I poured myself another drink.

"How do they manage it? Serial killers?" I asked Celeste once. "I can barely keep my shit together, and I only have one job." I was having a lot of days when things like showering and buying groceries seemed not only pointless but basically impossible.

"It energizes them," she said, without hesitation. "They're at work, they're waiting in line at the DMV, whatever, and they're thinking about what they've done, what they're going to do. It's how they get through the day."

Often violence is a kind of eruption, like Sara Morgan's murder. I thought of the beautiful Crawford campus, the little brick buildings, the manicured lawns covered in snow, the thin, clever students in their expensive winter shoes. Some of them would be talking about her in therapy for years, I knew. Even if they didn't know her well, their proximity to something so cruel would change their world. It would be like coming home and finding a wolf waiting for you in the living room, licking its paw.

But occasionally violence could be something else entirely. Sometimes an unthinkable, unforgivable act, or in Logan's case, a whole series of them, could make everything around it shine. I saw it for myself when I drove to his house, that terrible, ugly old house where he killed six women. There was nothing to distinguish it from any other ugly old house, except for the smell.

Still, it was as if all that death formed a kind of halo around the house. If I believed in ghosts, I might have thought it was the six women, hovering above, as if to say: *He kept us in his basement like so much trash. But look at us now. We're angels.*

I felt it again whenever I brought up the topic of Logan, the way even people like Sean, who knew so much better, got just a bit excited at the idea of what he did. Like there was glamour to it—glamour in the oldest sense of the word, a kind of illusion, an awful magic. As if killing six women were so terrible that it makes a person just slightly supernatural.

I should have known better, too.

When I heard the door open, I nearly broke my neck, leaping out of my chair to greet him.

"I'm working on a new article," I told him, as he took off his shoes and hung up his coat. "About this other murder, at Crawford."

"Christ. Another one?"

"Yeah. Unrelated. A college girl. Her boyfriend stabbed her." I knew he slit her throat. But "stabbed" was easier to say. You could keep a conversation going if you used the word "stabbed." "Slit" silenced a room.

"Fuck, Juliet. That's terrible."

Sean hung up his coat and filled the cat's bowl with food.

"At Crawford?" he asked.

"Yup."

"We played a show there once."

"Really? What was it like?"

"Fine. Weird kids, honestly."

"Yeah. That's the sense I got." I pressed my face against his shoulder. "I wonder if she was there. At the show."

"Who?"

"Sara. The girl who died."

"Oh. Uh, I don't know."

"No, I know. There's no way you would know. Of course. I was just wondering."

He frowned. That type of thinking irritated him. I wished that I had kept the question to myself. I could say that kind of stuff to Celeste, but not to him.

"This is good for you, though, isn't it?"

"What do you mean?"

"Like, for your career. 'If it bleeds, it leads.' Isn't that what they say?"

"I guess. But it isn't that kind of story."

"Why not?"

"Because we're not that kind of newspaper. We're a local paper, we do stories that are, I don't know, tamer." I heard a hitch of exasperation in my voice, and took a deep breath. "Besides, I want to be respectful."

"Of course. But still, it's not exactly the kind of story you can make family-friendly."

"No. I guess not." We sat down on the couch, and I leaned into him, relieved to feel his body make way for mine.

"I like that about you," he said.

"Hmm?"

"You know, that you take it seriously. That you still care about being respectful. Not everyone would."

"Oh. Thanks."

He shrugged and looked away. These scraps of kindness he handed me—I could gnaw on them for days.

Our cat, a tiny, capricious animal named Cat, dove onto his lap. A tabby who must have been the runt of the litter, she used to belong to Nell, Sean's girlfriend of several years before we met. Cat adored Sean and tolerated me. Cautiously, I leaned over to scratch behind her ears.

Sean turned on the television. "Pretty baby," he said to the cat.

We fucked right there on the couch, not even taking off all our clothes. Cat watched balefully from the coffee table. I liked having the television in the background. I found it relaxing. When it was over, I felt empty, and warm, and calm. Sean asked what I wanted for dinner.

"Anything," I said. Cat continued to stare at me.

We ate spaghetti with meat sauce. Sean cooked simply, but well, and I didn't realize until the food was in my mouth how hungry I'd been. The television was playing a movie with Gene Tierney.

"Didn't she go crazy?" I asked Sean, though I already knew she did.

"No idea."

"She was so pretty."

"Yes, she was."

"Not as pretty as Cat."

"No. No one is as pretty as Cat, though." He gave her a kiss between the eyes. She yowled and scurried off to a corner. I took our empty plates into the kitchen and returned to the couch. Sean pulled me onto his lap, and I rested my head on his shoulder.

When I was in high school, my father taught me how to shoot a gun. He took me to a range two hours from our house, and I stood in front of him, feeling small and brave. He taught me how to line up the barrel, how to stand, where to hold the stock so that it didn't hurt me when I fired. I found that hollow spot on Sean—just below his shoulder, skin easily revealing the veins beneath—and placed my head there.

We kissed for a while. He moved on top of me. I felt the pressure of his fingers on my throat. Was he pressing hard, or was I imagining it, my anxiety making me too tender?

I shifted out from under him and stood up.

"Hey. Hey, are you OK?" Sean looked stricken.

"Yes, I'm fine."

"Did I do something?"

"No, of course not. I just need to go to the bathroom."

I trudged upstairs. The tiles were the same shade of gray you often see in office buildings and state hospitals. *I hate this house*, I realized. It was so fucking ugly.

John Logan's trial lasted one more month. He pled guilty to avoid the death penalty and was sentenced to life in prison. There was cheering in the courtroom when the sentence was read. It made me sick, even though I understood why seeing someone bad punished sometimes felt good.

Celeste and I watched the families of the victims embrace one another and shake hands with the prosecutors. I felt like I was watching a movie I wanted to switch off.

"Our last romantic date," Celeste said, when we met at the diner. "How tragic."

"Heartbreaking," I agreed.

I told Celeste about the conversation with my mother. "She thinks Logan's victims got what they deserved," I paraphrased.

Celeste shook her head. "Lots of people I work with think like that. They think empathy is a limited resource, that they have to hoard it, only give it to those who need it the most—it's not. It's a muscle. You have to exercise it."

We sat in silence. I could not make myself eat.

"You look exhausted. Take some time off," she advised me. "Take a break from all this. Go to a spa."

"I can't afford a spa."

"OK, well. Take a lot of hot baths. You'll be fine."

It was painful to admit it, but there are some things that just can't be fixed, not by any quantity of pills or vacations or hot baths or yoga or meaningful talks with understanding friends.

"Are you disappointed in me?" I asked her.

"No," she said. "If you were really giving up, I would be. But you're not."

"And if I do?"

I stared at her.

"Why do you think you're so obsessed with her?" Celeste asked.

"Well, aren't reporters supposed to be obsessive?" I answered, petulantly.

"To a point. Look, if her family got in touch with you, saying, we want justice for our little girl, we want that bastard to rot in prison, whatever, that would be something else. But they didn't, did they?"

"No."

"That means they want to grieve in private. So let them."

Sara was survived by her mother, Christabel, her father, Richard, her stepmother, Colleen, and her half sister, Luna. None of them wanted to talk to me.

Celeste spoke with so much certainty, even about things I knew neither of us could ever really understand.

"You feel connected to her," Celeste said. Her voice softened. "You'll feel that way about other people you write about, too. Trust me."

"I told you, I'm going back to covering the Sheep and Wool Festival."

"So maybe you'll feel connected to a certain lamb. Who knows."

I put my head down on the table. Celeste stroked my hair.

"You need a break," she said again. "It's OK. I was the same way. I took it all so personally."

Outside the diner, we hugged and promised to keep in touch. I drove home, completely hollowed out.

Three weeks later, Odile called me to say that there would be a vigil to honor Sara Morgan, as well as John Logan's victims. Sean came with me. There were maybe fifty students there, gathered outside the library, holding candles. A handwritten poster read: HONORING VICTIMS OF GENDER-BASED VIOLENCE. It was decorated with flowers. A girl who introduced herself as the leader of some kind of activist group made an earnest, if uninspired speech, followed by a minute of silence. They sang "Over the Rainbow" and "Hallelujah," and then it was over.

I sat in my cubicle long after everyone else had left and wrote three hundred words on the vigil. It appeared below an article about a historic mansion that was about to be demolished, and above an ad for a babysitting service.

The next day, when it appeared in the paper, I cut it out and sent it to Celeste. A week later, she sent me a hand-written note on thick, elegant stationery that said: *I hope this gives you some much needed closure.*

I knew that was her way of telling me to move on. *Either do this job or don't. If you're going to cover Maritime Museum fund-raisers and local productions of* A Doll's House, *do it with your whole heart and brain. Otherwise, give up and go to law school.* I put her note back in its envelope and placed it in my file cabinet, right next to the sticky note with the names of Logan's victims. Then I locked the cabinet and drove home.

Sean was already in bed, reading a paperback.

"Rough day?" I asked.

"No, but tiring," he said. "And yours?"

"They sentenced him to life in prison. People were cheering."

"Wow," he said. I appreciated that he didn't attempt anything more profound than that. I crawled into bed next to him with my clothes and shoes still on.

"I'm exhausted," I told him.

"I bet."

"I want to sleep for a thousand years."

"But then," he said, "who will cover the Garlic Festival?"

"I'll send my ghost," I said.

He kissed my forehead and cheeks.

"Weird girl," he said. "At least take your shoes off."

"No," I said, so he took them off for me.

Cat watched us from the dresser.

"What are you reading?" I asked.

"A murder mystery."

"Really?"

"I'm kidding. It's about World War I."

"Even more fun."

"Do you want me to read to you?"

"Sure. I guess."

I pressed my face to his chest as he read. I listened to names, and dates, and deaths, and the steady sound of his breathing, until, finally, I slept.

Sam

He could have sworn it was her. The woman sitting next to him on the plane looked so much like Sara Morgan. As she leaned forward, reading a magazine, her dark hair obscured her face. She folded over a corner with a long finger.

The illusion lasted only a second, but it rattled him. When she looked his way, he gave her the same tight, polite smile that airplane passengers always exchange. He guessed that she was seven or eight years older than Sara had been when she died.

Sam was on his way home to Boston from San Francisco, where his mother now lived with his stepfather, a software engineer. The trip was pleasant. He and his mother got along well, San Francisco was beautiful, and the software engineer was perfectly nice. On the phone with his girlfriend, Jocelyn, he didn't have much more to say than that. He didn't know why the trip had exhausted him.

Maybe you're just getting old, Jocelyn had offered. She was twenty-four, studying for her master's in social work. She had a twenty-four-year-old's energy, and a twenty-four-year-old's perfect tits. She joked about their age difference a lot, trying to make it less weird. Sam was about to turn thirty-six. He was starting to think that if he married anyone, it might as well be Jocelyn. But thinking about that, too, made him tired.

He'd met her at an art show he was part of, contributing some oil paintings that he thought were his best work in a while. Jocelyn liked them, too. He hadn't done a lot of painting since they started dating, which he suspected was because he wanted so badly to impress her. It was paralyzing him. "Nothing in nature blooms all year," she said when he lamented his lack of productivity. At the time he found it a beautiful and profound statement. Now, having heard it from her at least a dozen times, he thought it was pretentious and fucking banal.

All of Jocelyn's friends thought he was a creep, which wasn't unfair. At first, he'd tried to win them over by being as charming as possible, and bringing decent wine to their shitty parties. "They don't care about that kind of stuff," Jocelyn finally told him. "Just be nice to me, and they'll like you." This didn't reassure him. At least no one could say that she was only with him for his money, because unlike most of the people he went to college with, he didn't have very much.

Sam texted Jocelyn to let her know he was on the plane and then turned off his phone. He started to read his book, a novel about World War II that his mother had given him. She usually had good taste, but Sam read without absorbing any real information.

"What's taking them so long?" asked the woman next to him. He wasn't sure if the question was rhetorical or not. He stared at his book.

Twenty minutes passed. The other passengers were restless. The woman was texting someone. The sound of her nails on her phone's screen put Sam on edge.

After forty-five minutes, a flight attendant informed them that there was a problem with the engine. There was a chorus of irritation and disappointment.

"We will of course provide everyone with accommodation for the night," the flight attendant added.

"Fuck you," a man said.

"It's not *her* fault," Sam said without thinking. The man didn't seem to hear him, but the dark-haired woman smiled.

"It can't be a fun job," she said to Sam.

He nodded. "You have to deal with people at their absolute worst, their most irritable."

"And entitled."

"Yes, and entitled."

He helped her get her suitcase down from the overhead bin. She didn't actually look like Sara at all, he realized. Her features were sharper, and she was taller. But now that the idea was in his head, he couldn't get rid of it.

As they exited the plane, he texted Jocelyn to let her know what was happening. She sent back a frowning face, and then: *I miss you.*

I miss you too, he replied. He spotted the dark-haired woman a few feet in front of him. He walked faster, until he was close enough to tap her shoulder.

"Have a drink with me?" he asked.

Sam and Blake were roommates their freshman and sophomore years of college. During their junior year they moved to a house off campus, which they shared with two other students.

It was difficult, afterward, to explain why they were such close friends. At the time Sam didn't give it much thought. The two of them just got along really well. They liked a lot of the same music and movies and were content to sit around smoking weed, talking about girls and philosophy and basketball. You wouldn't think a life-altering friendship could be built out of such mundane things, but it can.

Sam and Sara slept together about a year before she and Blake started dating. It wasn't that big of a deal. Everyone in their group of friends slept together at some point. Blake once joked that casual sex was the only sport at which Crawford students truly excelled. It was unfashionable to get jealous, to take it too seriously.

In the small Massachusetts town where he grew up, Sam was called a faggot, or ignored. At Crawford, girls loved his thin frame, his curly hair, his T-shirt with Walter Benjamin's face on it. He had a reputation as a womanizer, selfish, bad news, a possible sex addict, which he thought was unfair. He believed that he was a much more modern and enlightened kind of man than his father, a second-rate anthropology professor who left his mother for a TA.

At the time Blake and Sara started dating, Sam had just broken up with his most recent girlfriend, an impossibly beautiful sculpture major named Alison. For reasons he could not explain, even to himself, he had cheated on her mercilessly. One of the girls he slept with toward the end of the relationship was Lizzie, Sara's best friend. But Lizzie had known he had a girlfriend, just as Alison knew he slept around. It wasn't particularly nice of him, but Sam still didn't think he deserved the cold way that Sara treated him.

When he brought it up to Blake, it went badly.

"What the fuck are you even *talking* about?" Blake had asked.

"She's just kind of . . ." Sam struggled. It was true that she had always been unfailingly polite.

"If you think she's judging you, maybe that's your issue."

It was as close to a real fight as they ever got. Sam admitted that he was being paranoid.

Sam knew that Blake started taking antipsychotic medication in high school. Blake had revealed it early in their friendship, during one of their many late-night, alcohol-fueled conversations. Sam didn't take it very seriously at the time. A lot of the people he knew at Crawford were on one psychiatric medication or another. It wasn't until senior year that he realized Blake had a real problem. He found him in the kitchen at dawn, sewing Sara's name into the palm of his hand. Sam startled him, and Blake—accidentally, apparently—plunged the needle straight through his hand. Sam wrapped the wound in paper towels while they waited for the ambulance to arrive.

Sara met them at the hospital. She sat by Blake's side all night, still wearing her pajamas, clutching his uninjured hand in hers. They had only been dating for a few months, but under the cold fluorescent light, they looked like they had known each other for decades. Their bodies folded into each other's.

Blake's psychiatrist put him on new drugs that made him a little quieter and more tired than before, but otherwise he seemed back to normal. He and Sara started to spend all their time together. Theirs was a secret world. No one else was allowed inside. No one else was even allowed to look.

The dark-haired woman's name was Mary. "Boring, I know," she said.

"Not at all. Like, if I met an old lady named Mary, that's not a big deal, but you don't *look* like a Mary, so that makes it exciting."

Listening to himself talk made him want to bash his head into the wall. But he kept going.

"So what brings you to sunny California?" Outside the airport hotel, it was raining heavily.

She laughed, a pretty, girlish laugh he suspected was practiced. "Work."

"What do you do?"

"I'm a pharmaceutical rep."

"Really?"

"I know, I know. It's not exactly the most honorable job."

"It's not the least honorable job, either."

"I suppose not."

"Like, if we put it on a scale, ten being a war criminal, and one being, let's say, doctors without borders, a pharmaceutical rep is maybe, a five?"

"A five?"

He worried briefly that she was offended, that he should have said a three or a four. But she smiled.

"Is 'war criminal' really a profession, do you think?" she asked.

"Well, I imagine it eats up a good part of the day."

"Yeah, it's hard to believe they see it as a hobby."

"I wonder what the hours are like," he said. His second gin and tonic was making him reckless. "I wonder if they get lots of paid time off."

"Probably not. And the work–life balance must be hard. Great opportunities for growth, though."

Now he, too, was giggling. They went up to her hotel room.

During their sophomore year Sam and Blake started a literary magazine called the *Pine Street Review*, named after the street they lived on. They got all their friends to write poems for it, and Sara made the cover, a cyanotype of keys and leaves and a dead moth. One of their friends, who lived in a big old house off campus, hosted the release party. They decorated the living room with Christmas lights and wildflowers in small glass jars. Of course, the party and not the poems was the point of the whole endeavor.

The poems were, on the whole, pretty bad. Sam had not kept a single copy. What he did have in his possession was an edition of Crawford's student newspaper from the week that Sara was declared missing. The *Crawford Voice* was published monthly, and that issue contained, in addition to information about the case, a poem Blake had written, titled "For Sara."

& when i woke
all that was left—a shadow
of a memory of a shadow

i pressed my lips
bang against the paper.
i took a silver hammer
to the delicate machine
in my head. inside

a bird, its wings heavy with honey and ink—
a song so beautiful only you can hear it

By the time the issue went to print, Sara's body had been found, and Blake had confessed to killing her.

Sam told the police that he never saw Blake display any violent or misogynistic tendencies. He didn't consider the hand-sewing incident violent, because Blake clearly didn't want to hurt anyone else while he was doing it. And anyway, Sam would have lied for Blake, easily, even under oath.

There was only one other exception, and it didn't even come to mind until a couple of years after Sara's death. It was the last week of their junior year. Some friends of theirs were having a celebratory barbecue. Sam wasn't sure why so many of his classmates wanted to act like suburban dads, grilling hot dogs and standing around in flip-flops. Their friends had a big, long backyard that dipped into a creek. There were girls playing in the water. He saw Alison in a black bikini, laughing, her hair wet against her shoulders. When she caught him staring, she glared imperiously.

Sam spent most of the party with Blake and Sara. Blake was eating ribs and Sara was daydreaming. She leaned into him and he stroked her head, leaving drops of barbecue sauce in her hair. Lizzie was there, sort of hovering around Sara the way she often did, like a guardian angel or a baby-sitter. If it irritated Sara, she didn't show it.

By sundown almost everyone was drunk. A girl Sam didn't recognize came up to them, barefoot, swaying. She was probably someone's sister or cousin, in town for graduation.

"Wow," she said to Sara. "You are so beautiful. You are exquisite."

"Thanks," said Sara, bemused.

The girl wandered off. When she was out of earshot, Blake said: "She has a dog's face."

It wasn't exactly sexist, or even that cruel, but it stayed in Sam's mind because of the glee with which Blake had said it. Sam and Lizzie had made eye contact for just a second, and then both burst into laughter. It was such a strange thing to say, especially for Blake. There was no way to understand it except as a very odd, bad joke.

In Mary's hotel room, Sam felt the drinks wearing off, his exhaustion creeping in. He suggested that they have another drink out of the minibar, and she agreed. The tiny bottle of Sapphire gin in her hand made her look like a giant.

"You remind me of someone," he said recklessly.

"Who?"

"Someone I liked a lot."

"An ex-girlfriend?"

"No. No." He rested his hand on her thigh, the soft, dark fabric of her skirt. "She wasn't my girlfriend."

"But you wanted her to be?"

He didn't mean for her to take it seriously, to get so curious.

"Not exactly."

"What happened to her?"

"She was murdered, actually."

"Oh my God!" Mary's eyes went wide, revealing wrinkles Sam hadn't noticed before. The light in the hotel room was less forgiving than it was in the bar. "That's terrible."

"It is," he agreed.

"Why? What happened? Did they catch the person who did it?"

Sam sighed deeply. "I don't want to talk about it."

Mary frowned. "You're the one who brought it up."

"I know. I know." His hand was under her skirt now, her thighs cold from the air-conditioning. "I shouldn't have."

They kissed for a while. Abruptly Mary stood up. "Would you like some water?" she asked.

"Sure."

She got two heavy glasses from the bathroom and filled them with tap water. They sat and drank in silence. When his glass was empty, Sam kissed her again, and started to unbutton her shirt.

She moved his hands away, but continued to kiss him. This went on for a few minutes. Sam was irritated. He took each of Mary's cold, pretty hands firmly in his and placed them by her sides.

"Really?" she said.

"Really, what?" A headache started to pulse behind his temples.

"Is this really what you want to do?"

"To have sex? Yes. Isn't that why we're here?"

"I don't want to have sex with you."

"Fine. You could have said that."

"I am saying that."

He stood up. He could not remember the last time he felt so humiliated.

"You know," he said. "A person could get a little confused, after being invited to another person's hotel room. They might get somewhat puzzled."

"Is that so?"

"Yes, it is."

"And then that person might, in their confusion, do something like pin my hands behind my back?"

"What? I didn't do that."

"You just did!"

Sam had no idea how to respond. He was not a man who hurt women in hotel rooms. The whole thing felt like watching a bad television show, watching a character make terrible choices. It was unbearable.

"That wasn't my intention," he said, finally.

"I'm sure it wasn't." Her voice was quiet and very even.

They stared at each other. Finally she said, "I think you should leave. To avoid further confusion."

He did.

In the morning, Sam paid a stupid sum of money for an upgrade on his flight home, just to make sure he wasn't seated next to Mary. This time the person next to him was a grumpy man in an expensive-looking suit. Once the plane was safely in the air, Sam took two Valium, a parting gift from his mother.

He started to watch a movie but fell asleep twenty minutes in. The movie was about a gangster who wanted revenge against another gangster. The Valium made it hard to tell if the movie was supposed to be funny or not. It slipped into his dreams. In his dream, both gangsters were

Sara. One Sara had a gun, but she didn't know how to use it and wanted him to help. He kept saying he didn't know how to use a gun either, but his voice was too quiet for her to hear. *What?* she kept saying, getting louder and more irritated. *What?* The other Sara was approaching. Sam woke with a start as the airplane was touching down.

A week after Blake was released from the psychiatric hospital, Sam went to visit him. Blake's family was more or less what he imagined: kind, warm, worried. They gave him the guest room, down the hall from where the rest of them slept, with fresh towels folded at the foot of the bed and African violets growing in little terra-cotta pots by the windowsill. Blake was barely recognizable. He was skeleton-thin, despite the bowls full of healthy snacks that his mother kept bringing him, and his hair had been cut very short. Due to the new antipsychotics he was on, he spoke slowly, or not at all. Even if Sam had the courage to ask him what had really happened, Blake probably wouldn't have been able to answer. They spent the weekend watching television and going for walks around the neighborhood. On their walks, the Campbells' dog, Louis, whined and tugged at his leash because of how slowly they were moving. Sam was relieved when Monday arrived. He and Blake had not spoken since that visit.

Later that same month, Sam moved home to live with his mother. He got a job at a gallery in Boston. It took him an hour and a half each way to get to work. He passed the time by reading. He read more during his commute, he suspected, than he had during his entire college experience. He was especially interested in books about sociopaths. He learned about their typical traits. They were charming, had few inhibitions, and were often cruel. Blake was certainly charming, but so was Sam. He didn't have many inhibitions, but neither did anyone at Crawford. As for cruelty—didn't killing Sara speak for itself?

Sam knew that the judge ruled that Blake was temporarily insane when he killed Sara, which meant he didn't know that what he was doing was illegal. Sam also knew that Blake was on a lot of medications, even before he started college, and that he sometimes said incomprehensible shit or slept for days at a time. That, plus the acid the two of them had taken, could lead to a psychotic episode.

Everyone who mattered had decided that Blake was out of his mind and could not be held responsible for Sara's death. Sam had no reason to think he knew better. Still, he wondered if Blake could have fooled everyone. It was hard to imagine, but not that much harder than it was to imagine his best friend slitting Sara's throat.

What he hated Blake for, he had to admit to himself, was not just killing Sara but destroying every good memory he had of his college days. It was all poisoned. When Sam thought of the bonfire they made in the woods at dawn, the issues of the *Pine Street Review* they stayed up all night putting together, the parties they went to, the road trip they'd taken to an abandoned Christian theme park in Connecticut, he did not feel nostalgic or sentimental. He felt ill. Every good moment, every small adventure, was now colored by the knowledge of what Blake had done, of who Blake was. Even the image of sitting around their backyard at dusk, smoking weed, now felt sinister.

It was late when he got home. Jocelyn was asleep on the couch, a stack of papers on the coffee table beside her. She rose to kiss him, standing on her toes to meet his mouth. She really was absurdly pretty, Sam thought, maybe even prettier than the girls he slept with in college. She followed him into their bedroom. They fucked quietly, efficiently, and fell asleep. Around dawn, they woke and fucked again. Jocelyn made sounds like a dog being kicked.

In the morning, they slept late and went out to brunch around noon. It was Sam's idea, but Jocelyn picked the restaurant, a place a friend of hers had recommended. The white tablecloths and heavy silverware made him think of room service in a hotel. Jocelyn was wearing a blue dress and her hair in braids across the top of her head. They talked about her classes, her friends, the television shows they both liked, a movie she wanted to see. They both drank several glasses of good red wine. Sam didn't mean to bring up Blake, but he did. They had only spoken about him a few times, when they first started dating. It took Jocelyn a few seconds to recognize his name.

"Oh, shit," she said, when she did. "What made you think of that?"

"Not sure," Sam lied, pouring himself another glass of wine. "He's been on my mind lately. I guess I've never really dealt with what happened."

Jocelyn murmured sympathetically.

"It's fucked up," she agreed. "But you know, it happens. More often than you'd like to think. People take the wrong cough medicine and end up strangling their kids. The only thing more fragile than the body is the mind."

Where the fuck did she hear that? Sam wanted to know. Instead he said, "I've been wondering if he's a sociopath."

She nodded. "It's possible. I know a therapist who had a client who she says was a psychopath. He killed himself in her office. Like, hanged himself in the entryway, so that when she opened the door, there he was."

"Jesus."

"Isn't that awful? She actually had to go to therapy to deal with it. I mean, it's possible that your friend was a sociopath, but even if he was, it's not like you will *ever be able to figure it out. It's better to just let it go."*

Something about the way she said you *was so derisive, so unlike her.*

"Are you drunk?" he asked, irritated.

"What? Maybe a little." She shrugged. "We're celebrating your homecoming, aren't we?"

"You're not really paying attention to what I'm saying."

To hear himself talk like that was infuriating. He sounded like the idiot husband in a sitcom. Jocelyn giggled.

"Not paying attention?"

"Yeah. Like you're thinking about something else. Something you think is more important."

"And what could be more important than you?"

"That's not what I'm saying—come on, Jo."

"It is, actually, exactly what you're saying." She took a bite of her steak, chewed and swallowed primly. "When you want me, you want me to be yours, completely. And when you're busy, with work or your family or some other woman, you want me to cease to exist, so that you don't have to worry about me, or feel bad. It's OK. It's not a crime. I think it's what all men want, to some extent. You just need to know it isn't really possible."

He stared at her. She took another bite of her steak and washed it down with what was left in her wineglass.

"I just need a moment," she said, and got up from her seat. For a second he thought she would leave the restaurant, but instead she tapped on a waiter's shoulder to ask him where the bathroom was. Bits of her hair were coming loose from her braid, falling around her neck like worms.

Gemma

Gemma, her husband, Frank, and their daughter, Karla, live in the kind of town other Americans fantasize about. It's only an hour's drive from the Pacific Ocean, with low crime rates and excellent public schools. Its downtown shopping area resembles the small Maine town Gemma grew up in, except fancier, and earthquake-proof.

The Carson-Bailey School, called Sea-Bee by everyone, is in a gold-rush-era mansion, complete with an indoor pool and a ballet lawn. This morning, in the thick fog, it resembles a castle from a fairy tale.

Frank attended Sea-Bee when he was a child, and his fond memories of the community garden and interpretative dance classes convinced Gemma to send Karla there. Despite what Gemma sees as the profound silliness of its whole ethos, Karla seems to be doing well and is learning to read and tie her shoes as well as she would at a normal school. Gemma's worries were more or less assuaged until this week.

Gemma got a call from Karla's teacher, Lucia (all the teachers go by their first names at Sea-Bee), on Monday evening, and they scheduled a meeting for Tuesday afternoon. Gemma wanted to figure out the situation before alarming her husband. Lucia had referred to an "incident," but knowing Sea-Bee, that could mean that Karla had failed to properly appreciate her classmate's finger painting of a rainbow. Still, the tone of the teacher's voice made Gemma nervous.

They had agreed to meet in Lucia's classroom after school while Karla was in rehearsal for the school's expertly neutered version of *A Midsummer Night's Dream*. Karla, along with at least seven other first graders, is playing Mustardseed, clad in flesh-colored leotard and lots of yellow chiffon.

The classroom has a distinctly spa-like vibe, despite the claustrophobic array of art projects and writing assignments decorating the walls. As she enters, Gemma can smell lavender and sage. Because the holidays are approaching, the whole campus is covered in adorable secular decorations. Lucia's students have been making their own snowflakes out of cardboard and glitter glue. They hang from the ceiling with yarn. Gemma looks for her daughter's but can't find it.

It's cliché to talk about California's lack of seasons, but it really can mess with you. In the first few years she lived there, Gemma felt that she was losing all sense of the passage of time. She feared that if she closed her eyes, she would open them to find that she was three years old again, or eighty, or dead, or someone else entirely. After six years, the sight of trees in full bloom decorated with Christmas lights still made her slightly queasy.

Lucia is barely five feet tall, clad in red wooden clogs and the kind of peasant dress that was popular in the seventies. Gemma can see hints of tattoos on her wrists and the nape of her neck, little wisps of dark ink at the edge of her dress.

"Please have a seat," Lucia says, in a kind, slow accent that suggests she has never left California.

Gemma obeys, even though the only place to sit, other than the carpet, which is in the shape of a smiling giraffe, is a chair clearly meant for small children. She perches with her knees nearly at her chest and places her purse on the tiny desk.

"Thank you so much for coming in," says Lucia, serenely, folding herself much more gracefully into another tiny chair.

"Of course," Gemma answers. "What's going on?"

"As I'm sure you know, Karla is a very bright child."

"Thank you," says Gemma, even though the compliment is not for her. Something stirs in her mind, and she locates it immediately. "Bright child" was the term adults always used to describe her brother, Blake.

"Her reading, writing, everything, is on the very high end of what's expected at this age."

"We know." Frank already has big plans for Karla. Stanford, Harvard, maybe even Oxford. Gemma doesn't want to be one of *those* parents, but she's starting to see how they come into being, how a small clever person can engender these ideas in grown-ups.

"It's not totally uncommon for gifted children to have behavioral problems. Have you noticed anything out of the ordinary at home?"

"No," Gemma answers honestly.

"Really?" Lucia seems doubtful. "She's not withdrawn ever? What about temper tantrums?"

"Nothing like that."

"Really?" Lucia repeats.

Gemma stares at her, her open, pretty California face, and feels a sudden desire to strike her. To control herself, she applies some lip balm.

"Absolutely nothing."

Lucia sighs deeply and pulls out what appears to be a shoebox. She opens it. Inside, on a bed of white tissues, are a number of baby teeth.

"Are those Karla's?" Gemma asks before realizing that the quantity of teeth means they could not possibly all be from the same child.

Lucia's face is now pale, as if from pain. "She's been collecting them. From the other children. She pays them."

"How much?"

"What?" Lucia looks startled.

"Well, I'm wondering, you know, if she's maybe been stealing out of my wallet," Gemma says, though truly she is just curious.

"Ah. I think, ten cents apiece?"

Karla gets two dollars a week for allowance. That's a lot of teeth, Gemma calculates. At least a few mouthfuls.

"Do you have any idea why she's doing this?" Lucia asks.

"None," says Gemma. "Is she in trouble?"

"Well, it's not as if there are school rules against this."

"No, I suppose there wouldn't be."

"But it's very odd. It's unsettling."

"Kids do weird things. Didn't you?"

"Yes, but—there have been complaints from other parents."

At this, Gemma can't help but bristle.

"I should think they'd be glad that their kids have found a way to earn extra pocket money." She's talking bullshit, she knows. She puts on more lip balm.

"I'm just wondering," says Lucia, very carefully, "if this is a sign of something else."

"Like what?"

"I honestly have no idea. I recommend talking to a therapist. We have a child psychologist on staff here, of course, but maybe she can recommend someone who is more equipped to deal with this."

"Which is what, exactly?" Gemma can't help being so defensive. *Wouldn't anybody*, she thinks, *if a person was implying that their child was so fucked up she required special expertise?*

"I don't know. I think it's best to find out sooner, rather than later. Don't you think?"

"Maybe."

"Is there any history of this kind of thing in your family?"

Gemma's body goes cold. Her maiden name isn't on any of the documents for Sea-Bee, and even if it were, would Lucia really recognize it? Blake's story never made national news.

She really is young, Gemma observes, looking at Lucia's pretty, anguished face. Do the children recognize that, or are all adults the same kind of infallible, inscrutable creatures to them?

"I need to talk to my husband about this," she says, finally.

"Of course."

They both reach for the box.

"Well, she did pay for them," Gemma says.

Lucia opens her mouth, as if to argue, and then, perhaps thinking better of it, smiles sympathetically.

"As I said, she's an extraordinary little girl."

"Yes, I suppose so." Gemma tucks the box under her arm in order to shake Lucia's hand. She walks out with her head held high.

As soon as she gets back to her car, she locks the doors and leans her head against the steering wheel. She has never been a crier, except when furious, and the shaking feeling in her stomach makes her think she will cry now, but she doesn't. She just sits there for a very long time, until play rehearsal is over, and it is time to take Karla home.

Gemma dropped out of college when she was twenty and went to live in New York with some friends who were students at Columbia. One of them helped her get a job at a coffee shop on Amsterdam. She hated it, but she hated it slightly less than college. While working there, she met Frank. He was in his first year of a neurology residency. He asked her to marry him after they had been dating for six months. Gemma was worried that her parents would disapprove of the twelve-year age difference, but they adored Frank immediately. She suspected that they were relieved to have her future suddenly so secure. Gemma and Frank got married in 1995, in the backyard of her childhood home. Her mother planned a party so simple and elegant it was featured in several local newspapers and magazines. A year later Frank received a fellowship at Stanford, and they moved to California. Frank was delighted to return to the West Coast. In California, he once told her, it's practically a sin to be unhappy. It means you're doing something wrong. He said that like it was a good thing.

Gemma found out she was pregnant that spring. While her mother was in California, helping Gemma with the baby, they received a call from her father. In an eerily calm voice, he told them that Gemma's brother, Blake, had been arrested for the murder of his girlfriend.

Everyone looks at their child and imagines, with horror, the terrible things that might befall them. But Gemma looks at her daughter and imagines that she will be a terrible thing.

Of course, girls are less likely to be violent—out of ability, Gemma believes, not desire. Still, she was relieved when she found out her child wasn't a boy.

When Blake was a baby, Gemma treated him like a puppy or a favorite toy. As he got older, he liked to direct his sister and cousins in plays he wrote himself, which their parents dutifully filmed. He was a beautiful child, blue-eyed and brilliant, before his face was dulled and his speech slurred by the antipsychotics prescribed for him in high school.

He was off his medications when he killed his girlfriend. She was a sweet girl, until she wasn't, until she was dead and frozen, her head almost separated from her body, in a shallow grave near a stream. Once, Sara had spent her winter holidays with Gemma's family in Maine. She was almost silent unless she was answering a question or offering a compliment. Gemma remembered finding her annoying, but not for any particular reason. Maybe Sara had been trying too hard to make everyone like her, or maybe Gemma had just been in a bad mood when they met. She had always imagined her brother with someone a little more interesting—a girl with blue hair who made experimental films, or some kind of radical environmentalist type. There was nothing wrong with Sara, but she just wasn't special.

Now Blake lives with their parents, works at the info desk in their local library, and sees a psychiatrist four times a week. It's not the life any of them imagined for him, but it isn't prison, either.

The prosecutor agreed with Blake's lawyer that he was not guilty by reason of temporary insanity. Blake spent sixty days in a mental hospital in Peekskill. Gemma visited only once, giving him a set of jams and marmalades in doll-sized jars. The gift was confiscated, and Blake explained that the staff was afraid he might smash the glass jars and use them to hurt himself or someone else.

"You'd do that?" Even under the circumstances, the idea of someone using such innocuous objects as a weapon shocked Gemma.

"No, no, I wouldn't. But they have to be very careful, you see." He talked slowly, as if to a child. Gemma never visited him there again. She expected her parents to give her a hard time about that, but they didn't.

Of course they still love Blake. That's their job.

When she gets home, Gemma goes through her usual routine. She pats their dog, Miles, while she takes off her shoes and leaves them on the wooden rack by the front door. She puts her keys in the ceramic bowl on the kitchen counter. Then she goes to the fridge and pours herself a glass of white wine. Karla is playing an educational computer game in the living room.

Bored, Gemma goes to their pool house, which is where her parents will be staying when they visit next week.

It will be the first time they have done so, the first time in six years they have felt that it was safe to leave Blake alone for an extended period of time. They barely know their granddaughter. Understandably, Frank has not wanted Karla to go with her mother when she visits her family in Maine, which she rarely does anyway.

Her parents' impending arrival fills Gemma with anxiety. As sad as it has been, she has become used to the distance between herself and them. The qualities she used to admire in them—her mother's steadfast sweetness, her father's quiet and unshakable confidence—seem useless, if not ridiculous in the context of what Blake did. They are the parents of a murderer, yet they still see themselves as respectable, regular people, pillars of their small community. At Blake's hearing, her father wore the same suit he'd worn at Gemma's wedding. Her mother brought snacks.

And anyway, she has her own family now. To have her parents here feels like an invasion. But when her mother called to say they wanted to visit, she didn't know how to say no. She certainly has the space to host them.

The pool house is twice the size of the apartment she and Frank shared in New York. There is a bed that can be pulled down from the wall, a leather couch, a glass coffee table, and an enormous television. In preparation Gemma has stocked the bathroom with expensive little soaps and a porcelain vase full of dried lavender. It looks great. She lies down on the couch, staring at nothing, and considers her life.

What does she *do* all day? She goes to the mall, where she buys clothes for Karla, tiny beautiful things her own parents would never waste money on. She exercises, without enthusiasm, running on a treadmill or doing yoga by herself in her bedroom. She reads a lot, though she can never seem to remember what happened in a book after it's finished.

She paints. Her paintings are fine, but no one will ever mistake them for art. They would look fitting in a motel, or a therapist's office. She uses bright, pretty colors to portray rivers, flowers, and trees.

Is that really a life? She is always doing things to clear her head, like walking Miles or going to acupuncture. Clear it of what, and to what end? She imagines her brain as a porcelain bowl, bone white and cold to the touch.

Her phone makes a shrill sound. It's Frank, reminding her that they're going to their friends' house for dinner and that she's already late. She apologizes profusely. "I'm on my way now," she lies. She doesn't feel drunk at all, but before she leaves the house she sticks her finger down her throat and vomits into the toilet, just in case.

The last thing Gemma feels like doing is having dinner with George and Melissa. They have just moved into a new, beautiful house and are eager to entertain people. George and Frank went to medical school together. Gemma had liked his first wife, Flora. Everyone had. She had died of cancer two years ago. No one likes Melissa. Gemma feels sorry for her, but she still doesn't like her. Melissa acted, Gemma thought, like she was a lot younger than she was. Either it was an act, probably to make men like her, which was creepy, or she was actually that stupid.

George and Flora had a daughter together, Sophie Anne, who is one year older than Karla. She seems to be doing fine, all things considered. Melissa puts on *The Lion King* for them to watch in the den, which is something Flora would never allow. She would have insisted on imaginative play. But the way the house wraps around, the grown-ups can watch the children watching their movie during dinner, which is nice. Melissa has made some kind of lamb stew, which tastes all right. Gemma goes through the whole dinner on autopilot, drinking glass after glass of wine without feeling drunk at all.

"So, Gemma, what have you been up to lately?" Melissa asks. Gemma is as startled as if Melissa had stuck a fork through her hand.

"The usual," she says, finally, and Melissa seems satisfied.

They continue to talk about comfortingly banal things, like renovations, vacations, television shows the other couple ought to check out.

The girls come in to ask for dessert. Sophie Anne is wearing a white dress with a pattern of pink and green roses. It makes Gemma think of a photograph she had hanging in her first apartment. It was by William Eggleston, and it featured a pretty red-haired girl lying on the grass, eyes closed, with a camera in her hand. The girl looked happy and peaceful, but also like she might be dead. The photograph, still in its frame, is probably somewhere in the garage.

While Melissa gives the girls ice cream, Gemma helps clear the table. Frank and George remain in the dining room talking. Around nine o'clock they all say warm and polite good-byes.

They give Karla the choice of coming home in Frank's car or Gemma's. She chooses Frank. When they arrive home, he carries Karla up from the car. She wakes up in his arms. Gemma gets her into pajamas and into bed before realizing she forgot to make Karla brush her teeth. One day can't hurt that much, she decides. To help Karla drift off, Gemma reads to her from *The Secret Garden*. It's a book she herself loved as a child, but she hadn't remembered how weird it was. The heroine, Mary, doesn't even cry when her parents die. Gemma was shocked to read that this time around, and mentions it to Frank, who is unperturbed.

"Lots of children's books are weird. Roald Dahl was a huge anti-Semite," he offers.

Still, Gemma hopes reading to Karla will protect her, at least a little, against the temptations of video games and reality television. It's the same reason she bought Karla porcelain dolls with big glass eyes instead of Barbies. As she kisses her daughter's forehead, she thinks: all this time, and all this money, to pretend that our children live in the nineteenth century, except without polio.

She turns off the light in Karla's room, and then the light in the hallway. Gemma lives in a big, beautiful house, separated from the main road by half a mile of scrubby grass and paved dirt. At night, it is quieter than she would like, though both Frank and Karla are light sleepers.

Once the lights in the kitchen and living room are off, Gemma retreats to the study, a glass of white wine in her hand. She sits down at her husband's desk, opens up a search engine, and types in her brother's name. She can find only one article, from a small newspaper, titled VIGIL HELD FOR VICTIMS OF JOHN LOGAN, CRAWFORD MURDER, by Juliet Leonard. The picture of the vigil is blurry and dark, and the article is perfunctory. It mentions Blake's name only once, and that he had been found not guilty by reason of temporary insanity. Gemma's mother had hoped, against reason, that Logan might have been the one truly responsible for Sara's death. The fact that he was in jail when she was killed hardly deterred the belief. Gemma is sympathetic to her mother's delusion, but barely.

Women, the article informs her, are 25 percent more likely than men to be murdered by someone they know. The article also quotes a Crawford student named Odile Mendelssohn, saying, "We have to face reality in order to change it." Gemma searches her name, too, and finds that she is now a yoga teacher in Berlin, which doesn't sound at all like a bad life.

Gemma calls her mother's number. Who else can she possibly talk to about what Karla is doing? Who else could begin to understand? Hope rises in her as the phone rings. *You have reached Alice Campbell. Please leave your name and number . . .*

Gemma calls again, but hangs up after the second ring. It's better to have the conversation in person, she decides, already knowing that she won't, that she will never have the courage, and that even if she did, her mother could not help her.

She pours herself another glass of wine, then two, then four. Around midnight she begins to feel ill.

Gemma goes into the guest bathroom, locking the door behind her. She curls herself around the toilet, begging her body's forgiveness. The white tiles of the bathroom floor are beginning to gray, she notices. Soon they will need to be redone.

Serena

olleen is sitting in my office, her thin legs crossed at the ankles, looking distraught. I haven't seen her since her wedding, sometime in the nineties. Prior to that, when she was still a Faraday, we worked together at a law firm in midtown Manhattan. Shortly after Colleen left, I became an investigator for the firm. Five years after that, I opened up my own private investigation business. We didn't really keep in touch, so it's a surprise to see her now.

She's a pretty woman, a little frail-looking, but otherwise indistinguishable from any other Westchester soccer mom. I give her black tea in a paper cup.

"It's so good to see you, Serena. I'm really sorry that I haven't been better at keeping in touch. You look fantastic."

"It's good to see you, too. How can I help you?" I don't want her to waste her time being nice to me.

She takes a deep breath and hands me a picture that looks like it was taken for a school yearbook.

"This is my daughter, Luna."

I nod, vaguely remembering a birth announcement many years ago. The girl has blonde hair parted down the middle and is smiling gamely at the camera.

"How old is she?" I ask.

"Eighteen. Just. Her birthday was in August," says Colleen.

August, I write on my notepad. I could remember this on my own, but I think it makes people more secure to see me write things down.

"She's gone missing," Colleen tells me. "There's no sign of foul play, and she's technically an adult, so the police won't help us. We were hoping you could."

"I probably can, yes. Tell me a little more about Luna."

Colleen takes several deep breaths before continuing. "My husband, Richard. Did you ever meet him?"

"I think so."

"I'm his second wife. He had a daughter from his first marriage, Sara. She was killed in 1997."

"I'm so sorry to hear that."

"Luna was only two years old. Too young to remember, but, of course, something like that has an effect."

"I can only imagine." Often people come to me when what they really need is a decent therapist, but I'm not sure that's the case with Colleen.

"Luna was always a shy kid. Well behaved, even when she was a baby. When she was, oh, ten or eleven? She started going to this summer camp. Willow Creek."

I write the name down on my notepad. Colleen continues.

"It's a Christian camp, in New Jersey. Richard and I aren't religious. It wasn't our idea. Some of her friends from school were going. We thought, what harm could it do? She seemed really happy there. She went every summer, and then even became a counselor-in-training. Luna graduated from high school a few months ago. The eighteen-year-olds at Willow Creek have the option to go on this two-week-long retreat-type thing. Richard was nervous about that. He said it sounded like a cult." She paused, as if waiting for me to agree with her husband. I said nothing. She continued.

"Like I said, Luna's always been good. Good grades, nice friends, all that. We never even had to give her a curfew. I think it's because of Sara. She doesn't want to give us anything to worry about, right?"

"I understand."

"So it didn't seem right, I thought, to not let her go. When I drove to get her, she wasn't there. I spoke to the director of the camp," she tells me. "Her name is Loretta O'Neill. She's not . . . She doesn't seem all there to me. I spoke to her, maybe yelled at her, a little. I wanted to know where my daughter was. She told me, 'She's fine, she's safe, she doesn't want to see you. She's following a *different path*.' I called the police, and they spoke to Loretta as well. They said there's nothing they can do. Luna was supposed to start at SUNY Purchase a week ago."

"Luna's eighteen, right?"

"Yes."

"All right. Anything else you want to tell me?"

Colleen sighs.

"Luna's hair is blonde, like mine. Just before she left for her retreat, she came home from a sleepover with it dyed brown."

"I don't understand."

"Sara's hair was brown," says Colleen. "Luna just looked so much like her. I thought Richard was going to have a heart attack. But he just walked out of the room."

"Sara, you said she was . . ." I struggle to put it politely. "That she was murdered."

"Yes. By her boyfriend. Blake Campbell."

I write down the name. "Is he still in prison?"

"No. He didn't go to jail. He was found not guilty by reason of temporary insanity."

"I'm so sorry," I say again.

"It was hard for Richard. For all of us. But especially . . ." Her eyes widen. "Do you think he has something to do with this?"

"No, no, that's very unlikely. I just need to follow up on all possibilities. OK?"

I take down all the rest of the information she can give me. The names and phone numbers of Luna's friends, her height and weight, blood type, allergies. Most of those things won't matter, but I want Colleen to feel that I am being thorough. She hands me a small stack of photographs. Luna and a group of friends all dressed as Disney princesses, carving pumpkins. Luna on a soccer field, her face distorted with determination. Luna at her debutante party, thin arms in white satin gloves. Luna at her graduation, flanked by her grinning parents.

"Do you think you can find her?" Colleen asks.

"Yes," I say, truthfully. Next to adultery, the missing sons and daughters of nice suburban families constitute the majority of my livelihood. "But the sooner I start, the better. I'd like to drive out to Willow Creek tonight, actually."

She hands over the check immediately.

Richard Morgan's first wife, Christabel, Sara's mother, is a psychic in western Massachusetts. She sells healing air plants and amethysts at exorbitant prices on her online store. Whether she's always done this, or if it's her way of coping, it's not my job to figure out. She and Richard divorced in 1989. I doubt Luna would go see her, but I place a sticker on my map anyway.

I put another sticker on the town in Maine where Blake Campbell grew up, and now lives, working at a library. Just in case. But I start at the most obvious place, Willow Creek.

Because a private investigator who drinks is such an unforgivable cliché, I take pills. They are given to me by a psychiatrist on West Ninety-Seventh Street. He's Harvard-educated, very well dressed, and so uninterested in me I doubt he could pick my face out of a lineup. He gives me a stimulant often used by the air force, Modafinil, ostensibly to help with the fatigue caused by my depression. The first week I took it, it made me so agitated, I thought I was going to strangle my dog. Now it works pretty well. I take fifteen milligrams, fill my car with gas, and drive to New Jersey. My dog, Capote, sits in the passenger seat, panting joyfully out the open window. He looks more like a wolf than household pet, which is occasionally useful.

The Willow Creek property is two and half hours outside New York City. Its website boasts of horseback riding, archery, and Christ. It's almost winter now, and the campus is eerily empty. I leave Capote in the car with the windows rolled down and walk to the main building.

A guy is sitting behind a fake wooden desk, clicking absentmindedly at a computer. When I walk in, he nearly jumps. I'm probably the first person he's spoken to all day.

"Welcome to Willow Creek," he says, recovering.

I show him my badge. Often people ask to see my license as well, but he's just a kid. At the slightest suggestion of authority, his face goes white.

"I'm looking for Luna Morgan," I say.

His eyebrows go up.

"We're committed to protecting the privacy of our community members," he says, robotically. Someone, I am sure, has instructed him to say exactly that.

I get out my wallet. I have a hundred dollar bill, but looking at the guy's T-shirt, stained with ranch dressing, I suspect it will be excessive. I put two twenties on the desk.

"How about a forwarding address?" I ask.

He stares at the money. He can't be older than nineteen. I wonder if he and Luna were ever friends.

He scribbles on a purple sticky note and gives it to me without meeting my eyes.

"The Wilsons. They used to come here when they were kids. They run an antique store outside Norton Hill. Nice people, and they always need spare hands."

On my way to Greenville, I stop at a rest area on the Taconic. Capote and I do a few laps around the parking lot to stretch our legs. I buy a bottle of water and a pack of M&Ms. In the bathroom, someone has written on the wall: YOU FEEL EMPTY BECAUSE YOU ARE. Below that, in tiny red letters, someone else has written: I FUCKED YR MOM.

"Antique store" is a nice term for the Wilsons' property. It's a junkyard. Just looking at their stuff makes me want to get a tetanus shot.

"Can I help you?" A girl dressed in shorts and a man's T-shirt appears. Her hair is dark, except for a halo of light roots.

"Luna Morgan?"

"Yeah," she says, without thinking. And then: "Who are you?"

I show her my badge. "You're not in trouble. Your parents have sent me to make sure you're safe."

"I am."

"I can see that," I tell her, making my voice gentle. "But I wouldn't be doing my job if I didn't ask you a few questions."

"Like what?" She crosses her thin arms across her chest.

"Why don't I get you a coffee? Is there somewhere nearby we can go?"

"Depends what you mean by nearby."

The closest coffee shop is in downtown Greenville, a brightly lit place twenty minutes away from the house. It has lots of glass and metal.

I can't have caffeine with my meds, so I order peppermint tea. Luna gets a latte and a chocolate croissant, which she consumes in two bites.

"Food isn't great there, I'm guessing."

She shakes her head.

"Why don't you order some more stuff? To take back with you?"

"Really?"

"Don't give me that look. I'm billing it all to your parents."

She laughs. "In that case, definitely."

I wait while she eats another croissant, and a blueberry muffin.

"It's cool that you're like, a female detective. I think my mom told me about you once."

"Investigator, not detective. I don't work for the police."

"Still." She tilts her head. "Do you carry a gun?"

"In my car. Not on my person."

"And the dog?"

Capote is tied up outside the café, napping peacefully. "He just keeps me company."

We stare at each other for a while. It's a trick I learned from psychiatrists. People hate silence and will start talking just to make it stop.

"So I guess I'm supposed to tell you why I'm here," she says, finally.

I shrug. "Actually, that's not part of my job. Though I am curious."

"You know about Sara, right?"

"A little."

"She died when I was two. I don't remember her at all. But when I was like, ten, eleven, I started having these horrible dreams. And I couldn't always tell what was real and what wasn't. I would tell my parents stuff like, *Sara is my substitute teacher.* Or I saw her at the supermarket. I'd see a girl in a magazine ad and be like—there she is! In retrospect, it must have been, like, fucking awful for my dad."

I nod.

"But not your fault."

"No, it wasn't." Her eyes narrow. "They put me on medications."

"Which ones?" I'm always very curious about other people's prescriptions.

"God, I don't even remember. My mom told me they were vitamins. I know I was on lithium at one point. That was the worst."

"Jesus."

"Yeah. And they didn't even really work."

"That would make me hate my parents, too."

She looks at me in surprise. "I don't hate them. At all."

"Really? Typically, that's what running away indicates."

"I know. And I know they're probably furious."

"Worried, more like."

"I just need space."

"From them?"

"No, from her. From Sara. I don't see her anymore but I still . . . feel her. Like a string tied around my throat."

"Your mom said that when you dyed your hair, it made you look like her."

"Yeah," Luna answered. She seemed embarrassed.

"Why?"

"If I could explain," she said, "I wouldn't have done it."

I pretend to sip from my empty tea cup.

"Do you feel better now?" I asked.

"What's that thing people say? 'Wherever you go, there you are'?"

"I think I've heard that once or twice."

"I guess it's, 'Wherever you go, there you are, and there's your dead half sister,' too. But it's easier. Not being in that house, with my parents. I'm a little bit more free."

What could I say to that?

"So, what now?" she asks. "Are you going to tase me? Throw me in your truck, take me back to Westchester?"

"No. Technically, that would be kidnapping. Also, your parents paid me to see that you're safe, not to bring you home."

"Oh." She seems genuinely surprised by this, but recovers quickly. "So, like, are you going to take a picture of me holding today's newspaper?"

"I was thinking of a video," I said. "My phone will time-stamp it. Just you saying hi, saying something to let them know you're OK."

"All right. Do we have to do that now?"

"I guess not."

"I need time. To think of what to say."

"How about I come by your house this evening? Is that enough time?"

"Yes. That's fine."

I drive her back to the Wilsons'. As she unbuckles, I notice that she's shaking slightly. Before I can think better of it, I say: "You don't really want to go back there, do you?"

"Not particularly," she answers, lightly.

"What's it like?"

"Not that bad," she says quickly. "They're nice. Really religious."

"I thought you were, too."

"I was, I guess. For a little while. I don't think it's exactly my thing."

"Understandable. But they're not hurting you or anything, are they?"

"God, no. It's just . . ." She gestures at the decrepit house and the desolate landscape that surrounds us. No eighteen-year-old wants to be here.

Finally, I tell her: "I could drive you to—what's the nearest real town?"

"There's an Amtrak in Hudson."

"I could drive you there. Where would you go?"

She thinks for a moment. "One of my friends moved to Philly a few years ago. Her parents are nice. They'd let me stay there for a little while."

"And then?"

Luna shrugs. "I'll figure it out."

She probably will.

"OK. Get your stuff and we'll go."

She disappears into the house and returns with a duffle bag and a raggedy blue backpack. It's probably the same one she used for school.

We listen to the radio on the way to Hudson. The drive takes almost an hour. Capote puts his head in Luna's lap as she stares out the window, patting him absently.

As we approach the station, she looks at me with an expression I can't read.

"Why are you helping me?"

I take a deep breath.

"I was like you once. A lost girl."

Luna shakes her head. "But I'm not lost. I'm running." She doesn't look at me when she says it.

"Either way. I was dependent on the kindness of strangers."

This seems to satisfy her. She slings her backpack over her shoulder. Capote whines.

"Got everything?"

"Yup."

I hand her my card. "Give me a call in a couple of days, let me know where you are. I won't tell your parents. I just need to let them know you're safe."

She hesitates. *You owe me that much*, I want to say, but then she takes it.

"Thank you," she says, quietly, and then walks off into the great dead heart of the country.

.   .   .

I dial Colleen's number. She picks up on the first ring. I give her the information for the train her daughter was planning on taking.

"I suspect she'll come home within the week," I tell her. "If not, give me a call, and I can go after her."

Colleen's voice is shaky. I suspect she's crying. "I know her friend in Philadelphia. She's a nice girl, her parents are nice people."

"That's good."

"At least she's not with those terrible church people anymore."

"No, she's not."

"Thank you, thank you, thank you."

"Just doing my job. Like I said, let's follow up next week."

"Of course. Thank you. Thank you . . ."

I let her repeat it a dozen more times before I tell her that I have somewhere to be, and hang up.

Tracy

When Tracy gets home, Erin is asleep in front of the television, underwear on inside out. A T-shirt with Billy Idol's face on it is pulled tight around her belly, revealing the white scars that decorate her hips. The television, which is playing a commercial for car insurance, is the only source of light in the living room.

It's tempting, like it always is, to just leave her there. Tracy wets a paper towel and uses it to wash her sister's face, gently, gently. Erin wakes with a low groan.

"It's OK, it's OK, it's just me."

"Tired," says Erin.

How can you be tired when you sleep all day? Tracy wants to ask.

"I know," she says. "But you need to sleep in your bed. The couch is no good for your back."

Erin doesn't move.

"Come on," says Tracy. She places her hands under her sister's armpits and tries to lift her.

"Good luck," Erin says, dully. "I'm way too fat for you to carry me."

"So get up and walk there yourself."

"God, why do you care?"

"Because you'll be up at three in the morning, and then you'll wake me up." Because it's depressing, the sight of her on the couch, because it makes Tracy fucking sad.

"I won't wake you. Just leave me be."

"Fine. This is a waste of my time."

"I agree," says Erin, closing her eyes.

Tracy heads upstairs to her room. It used to be her mother's room, and though she's redecorated it as much as possible—blue wallpaper with white dots, a white desk by the window, framed posters of Marilyn Monroe movies—every time she walks in, she expects to see her mother, dead these past three years, sitting on the bed, brushing her long dark hair.

Erin is the reason that Tracy became a prosecutor in the first place. She even wrote about her in her law school application essay. She did so against the recommendation of her undergraduate adviser, an American history professor who seemed to think of himself, for reasons Tracy never truly understood, as a type of father figure to her.

"It might be too controversial."

"Controversial, how?" she asked, playing dumb, which was not a strategy she often employed.

"Writing about that kind of thing, it comes across as confrontational, you know, maybe a bit aggressive. And also quite personal, of course. You wrote such a good essay last semester on *Coker v. Georgia*, perhaps you could use part of that?"

That kind of thing. He couldn't even say the word *rape* out loud. Tracy thanked him for his advice but didn't follow it. For the rest of her life, she would continue to think about him with pity and disdain.

Erin is sad, but Tracy is angry enough for the two of them. Rage has sustained her for thirty years. Other people would burn out doing this job. Tracy just burns.

She opens the window to let in some air and turns on the radio. Mendelssohn wafts through the room, tinny but still beautiful. Tracy takes off her shoes and her bra and lays her files out on the bed. She knows that she will not be able to sleep until she's finished reading this report.

Someone told her a long time ago that she shouldn't work in bed, that it confuses the body and makes it difficult to sleep. But it is the place in the world she feels the safest, with its locked door, her big dog sleeping on the floor. She puts on her glasses and spreads the papers across her pillow.

A college student was murdered by her boyfriend, a schizophrenic whose friend said that they had all done acid together the day the girlfriend went missing. The boy's lawyer is pushing for not guilty by reason of temporary insanity.

Tracy's instinct, regarding the NGRI, is: *Fuck no*. The victim, Sara Rose Morgan, was found after two days, her throat cut so deeply she was nearly decapitated. The defendant, Blake Campbell, is a boy from a nice family with an expensive lawyer, and though Tracy will do her best to keep this from prejudicing her against him, it does, a little. A young woman is dead for no reason, and someone ought to be held responsible.

But the court-appointed psychiatrist states that the boy is severely schizophrenic, his grip on reality tenuous at best, that he hears voices and instructions from gods and gurus. He has no prior history of violence. According to friends of both Campbell and Morgan, they were happily in love and talked about getting married.

When Tracy watched the tape of his confession—sobbing, saying over and over again that he just loved her too much, it was unendurable—she felt a flicker of that old anger. *If you loved her, you wouldn't have killed her*, she wanted to say, even though, of course, people kill people they love all the fucking time. She wants a more precise word than *love*, a better definition, one that doesn't allow for cutting anyone's throat open.

Campbell's lawyer is well known for his ability to make dead girls despicable, but he'll have a hard time with Sara, with her 3.8 GPA and her big brown eyes. From what Tracy knows, Sara never got a parking ticket or a grade below a B. Which doesn't mean Campbell's lawyer can't still turn her into a dumb slut, or a conniving succubus, or whatever he thinks will persuade the jury that she deserved to die. But if Campbell is truly insane, none of that matters.

Tracy is handling Campbell mostly by herself while the rest of the District Attorney's office focuses on the John Logan case.

She was doing dishes when she got the call from the Poughkeepsie police department that led her to interviewing a serial killer. Just hours after being arrested, Logan, for reasons perhaps best known to himself, asked to speak to a prosecutor. Tracy was the only one they could get in touch with on a Sunday morning.

The confession took nine hours. He told her how many women he killed, and why, identified their photographs, and explained where he hid the bodies. At the end, Tracy cried, humiliatingly, while a cop she didn't know held her tightly.

She cried for about ten minutes, then cleaned herself up in the bathroom, refused the cop's offer of a ride, and drove home. By the time she got there, a terrible, intoxicating thought occurred to her—that it was incredibly unlucky that she was now, technically, a witness, because prosecuting Logan would have been great for her career.

"Everyone loves a serial killer," said Erin, wisely, when she found out. "I would know. I watch TV all day."

It was hard to argue with that.

The Logan case was devouring the DA's time and resources. Even though Logan confessed, a jury still had to decide whether to execute him.

A sound from downstairs startles her. Tracy goes down to see what's going on. It's just a particularly loud commercial for Applebee's. She turns the volume down slightly. Erin is still asleep, though she's kicked her blanket to the floor. Tracy leans down to pick it up.

The blanket is made out of soft fake velvet. It barely covers Erin's body, all the pinkish flesh spilling out of her clothes. For just a second, Tracy allows herself to despise her sister.

Erin has not had a boyfriend, has not been on a date, since that night thirty years ago. *At least I won't die a virgin*, she once said.

The boys who raped Erin were Eliot Karr, seventeen, Larry Reid, eighteen, and Anthony Fox, seventeen. Karr lives in San Francisco, works in advertising, and is twice divorced, with no kids. Reid is an anesthesiologist in New Mexico, where he lives with his wife and twin daughters. Fox died in a drunk-driving accident when he was twenty-three. Tracy saw the photos. His car looked like it was turned into scrap metal.

Rape isn't about sex, an assistant DA had said to her recently. They were discussing the case of a teenage girl who had been assaulted by her friend's father during a sleepover. The ADA sounded so smug when he said it that Tracy wanted to slap him. Actually, she wanted to rip his throat out with her teeth. It was such a stupid thing to say. What made him think rape was about anything? It was like debating whether murder was about death. Ultimately the case never went to trial, because the girl refused to testify. Tracy didn't bother trying to convince her. She doubts they would have won anyway.

Because winter marks the anniversary, this time of year is hard for Erin. The lights strung in trees and the carols played in stores must remind Erin of how excited she had been for Winter Formal, of buying a dress from Nordstrom with the money she saved from babysitting. Larry was her date. He brought her a corsage, red roses that clashed with her pink dress.

What happened to her sister was terrible, but worse things have happened to people. In fact, Tracy has met some of those people. As an ADA, Tracy has worked with a woman whose drug dealer cut off her hand as a punishment for a missed payment, a teenage girl whose father chained her to a radiator, and the father of a boy who was killed and partially eaten by his gym teacher. They are fucked up, but at least they're still functional. They haven't forfeited their lives to fate the way Erin has.

Who knows, maybe Erin would have turned out like this anyway, even if she had never met any of those boys. Maybe she is exactly who she is meant to be.

According to the psychiatrist, Campbell's psychosis was severely exacerbated by his use of LSD. *If you're already schizophrenic*, Tracy thinks, irritably, *shouldn't you* not do drugs that make you even crazier?

If Tracy wanted to, she could take some of Erin's sleeping pills, but they might make it hard to wake up tomorrow. Instead, she allows herself a single Xanax. Erin, if she notices, will understand.

Because she takes pills so rarely, the Xanax hits Tracy hard, and she falls asleep with her clothes still on, the files next to her on the bed. She wakes up to Erin looming over her.

"What's wrong?"

"Nothing," says Erin, and laughs a little. "I came to check on you. I thought you were dead."

"Why would you think that?" snaps Tracy.

Erin shrugs. "Worked yourself to death, maybe?"

"Did you have a bad dream?"

"Yes. But not that bad."

"Do you need anything?"

"Nope. Just wanted to say hi."

Tracy rubs her eyes with the back of her hand.

"Can I sleep here?" Erin asks.

"If you want." Tracy gathers her files and puts them in a pile on her desk. "I haven't showered, though."

"I can tell." Erin curls up next to her. Tracy strokes her soft hair. When they were kids, their mother let them watch TV in her bed whenever they were sick. It was such a treat then. "Is everything OK with you?"

For a moment she considers lying: *I can't sleep, I'm afraid, I see dead girls out the corner of my eye*. Let Erin know that she's not the only person who suffers. But she decides against it.

"Work is just fucking exhausting."

"I bet. It's a lot to deal with. For anyone. Even you."

Even you. She means this as a compliment, Tracy thinks. Even someone as tough and smart and strong as you would be shaken by a serial killer.

"It's not Logan that's getting to me," she admits. "It's this other case. The Crawford kids." Out loud, "Crawford kids" sounds so silly, like a series of books about orphans who solve mysteries.

"Oh yeah? I'm not sure you told me about that."

"College girl's boyfriend slit her throat, left her in the woods to die. He's a diagnosed schizophrenic. Defense is saying he was having a psychotic episode, didn't know what he was doing."

"Do you believe them?"

"I don't want to. I want to believe that this guy is another spoiled brat who thinks he can do whatever he wants to women, and then I want to put him away for the rest of his life. But shit, what if he really . . ." Tracy's cheeks are getting warm.

"What if he really didn't mean to hurt her?"

"Yeah. Either he did know what he was doing, and now he's pretending, in which case he's an evil motherfucker. Or he really didn't know what he was doing, in which case he's . . ." Tracy gnaws on her thumbnail. "There isn't even a word for it. Imagine it's true. Imagine you really lost your mind, and then you come back to reality and your girlfriend's dead and you're the one who killed her."

"It's a nightmare," Erin answers. "Everyone knows bad things happen to good people—that's just life. Good people doing bad things, that's what's really scary."

Tracy sighs. "If I get all philosophical about it, I'll probably lose my mind."

"I really think you should talk to someone."

Tracy bristles.

"I'm talking to you, aren't I? And I'm not *actually* losing my mind."

"Why are you mad at me? It's just a suggestion. I'm trying to be helpful."

Her thumbnail is now bleeding. Tracy sucks on it. "I'm just tired."

"I'm sorry you're having a hard time. I just want you to be OK."

"I know." Erin curls up with her back next to Tracy's waist. Tracy strokes her hair until Erin is snoring softly. Then she creeps downstairs to the kitchen.

She pours herself a glass of water and drinks it while staring out the window into the dark nothingness. Then she calls Larry Reid. She has had the number written on a sticky note in her office for so long she has memorized it, though this is the first time she's actually dialed it. She presses the numbers slowly, making sure each one is correct.

She suspects that he'll deny it, just like he did thirty years ago. *I'm sorry she's having a hard time*, he will say, *but I never touched your sister.* Or worse: *I did touch her, but only because she wanted me to.*

But what if he apologizes? After all, the world is changing, isn't it? Maybe somewhere along the way, he realized what he did. That does happen. Tracy sees it all the time. Maybe he's been waiting for this phone call, for a chance at absolution. He will say: *I am so sorry. Please ask her to forgive me.*

And Tracy will say no. She will say, *We live with this burden, so you must, too. This is a debt that cannot be repaid.*

The phone rings three times.

"Hello," says Tracy. Her throat hurts.

"Hello? Who is this?"

It is a young girl's voice: high, sweet, confused, unafraid. Tracy hangs up the phone.

Jessica

October 8, 2000

Dear Mr. Logan,

As an assignment, my English teacher made us write a letter to a person living or dead, who we admire, and ask them some questions. I wrote to Buzz Aldrin and asked if after he came back from space our world was a letdown. But the person I really wanted to write to was you. So I am.

I don't exactly admire you (sorry!) but I do have some questions only you can answer. The big one is about Sara Morgan. She was my babysitter for four years. She looked after me and my sister Maggie. After she went away to college she still took care of us sometimes during the summer. She was murdered in 1997 and I want to know if you're the one who killed her.

I know that you are in prison for the rest of your life anyway so it doesn't really matter if you did or didn't so I hope you will just tell me. I won't tell anyone else. I know you don't necessarily believe me but I actually won't. I just want to know. The newspapers said her boyfriend killed her but he didn't go to prison and there isn't very much information about it. I have spent a LOT of time looking!

The reason I think it might have been you (no offense) is that Sara was pretty and dark-haired like your victims and she was killed in December 1997 and you were arrested that same month. I don't know the exact dates though like I said I have been trying really hard to find out!

I know you probably think I am some dumb girl and I hope I am not annoying you but please just tell me? If you say you did I won't judge or anything not that I think you would care but also if you say you didn't I will believe you.

Sincerely,
Jessica

October 20, 2000

Dear Mr. Logan,

My full name is Jessica Alison Keeler. My sister Maggie is two years older than I am. Sometimes people think we are twins. I had a brother too but he died when he was a little baby. I don't remember him but I get sad when I think about him.

Sara was a really good babysitter. Maggie and I both liked her. She was really pretty and she let us do our own thing. Once she let us watch Candyman because it was on TV and she got in a lot of trouble with our mom because Maggie got nightmares. I didn't. I like scary stuff.

Maggie was the one who told me about Sara. My mom didn't. I think she was hoping I'd kind of forgotten about her, and that I wouldn't someday be like, "oh hey what happened to that cool girl who looked after us" and she'd have to say "oops, sorry, forgot to tell you, some dude killed her." Maggie found out from her sister's friend who went to a college close to Sara, which is how she also found out about you. They did a big vigil for victims of male violence or something?

Maggie came into my room and closed the door behind her. She sat on my bed and held both my hands in hers while she told me. She seemed like she was about to cry but she didn't, and neither did I. I didn't know how I was supposed to feel. Sara was cool but it's not like I knew her so well. The interesting thing was Maggie acting like a big sister, or like she saw some big sister act in a movie, saying stuff like you have to be careful, it's a scary world out there, and I was like . . . I'm aware, thanks?

You asked if I am lonely. I never thought of it before but now I think you might be right. I do not think I am a freak but I think most other people would if they knew anything real about me. So I have friends but not really. But no I don't want to hurt anybody not even animals. There was a boy in my elementary school who tied a fire-cracker to a dog's tail. When I heard about it I cried and threw up. Here are my questions for you:

1. When you were a kid, what did you think you would be when you grow up?

2. What is it like to kill someone?

3. Do you ever get bad dreams?

Sincerely,
Jessica

December 2, 2000

Dear Mr. Logan,

I go to a catholic school that is girls-only and super strict. It costs lots of money so I'm supposed to be grateful to be there but I absolutely am not. The nuns act like if you have even one moment of fun in your whole life you will go to hell.

I'm on the soccer team but it's JV so no one cares not even us.

Teenage girls are supposed to have best friends. In the movies but also in real life. There's always one girl who leads, and one who follows. One who knows just a little bit more about the world generally, and she shows the other one how it's done. I don't have a best friend. I have some girls I call if I need help with homework and that's really it. When we were little I think Maggie was my best friend. But as she got older my mom made her look after me more and that probably sucked.

If I had a best friend, I would probably tell you that she dared me to write to you. And then when you wrote back we would read them together, in secret.

What were you like when you were a teenager? I bet you were one of those kids who never did any work but still got kind of good grades.

I have a lot of dreams about getting pushed down the stairs. I don't know why.

Do you ever feel sorry for the girls you killed?

Sincerely,

Jessica

December 22, 2000

Dear John,

You're right I will be getting my driver's license soon. Hopefully! It took Maggie like three times to pass her test, the big idiot. Anyway when I do I could MAYBE come visit you but I don't think so because it's far away and also my mom would freak out. Sorry.

I've been hanging out with this guy Derek. I think you would like him because he's really smart. Not smart like takes a bunch of advanced math classes or whatever but just gets stuff not everyone gets. I even told him about you. He asked if he could see your letters and I said I would ask you first. So can I?

Derek's sister Caroline is on my soccer team. He came to pick her up one day and we talked a little bit. He used to go to a college in Iowa but got kicked out for doing "too much acid, not enough homework"—his words. Now he's at community college. Caroline has always been my least favorite team member, always trying to make us wear ribbons in our hair for matches like we're fucking cheerleaders, so it surprised me that her brother was cool.

He offered to give me a ride home. Caroline sat in the backseat talking about whatever the whole time so it wasn't exactly romantic but I could feel him looking at me. That felt really good.

I have only kissed one person, at summer camp, a guy named Fred. After we kissed Fred said to me, "wow you really suck at this" which was a) mean and b) now that I think about it, actually HE was the one who sucked, using his tongue like it was some kind of a weapon.

I guess you can't really see it in the picture I sent you but my hair is super long, down to my waist! I brush it 50 times in the morning and 50 times at night.

Best,
Jessica

January 3, 2001

Dear Mr. Logan,

I told you, I've only ever kissed one person. There isn't even anything else to tell. And if there was I probably wouldn't tell you. Sorry!

When I was in elementary school one day I heard about a girl at the high school who hit a little kid with her car and he died. They arrested her while she was sitting in class. That story scares me so bad. I'm so afraid I'll do something terrible without meaning to and my whole life will be over. Does it make me a bad person that I feel bad for the girl who did it but not really for the little boy? Anyway that's my biggest fear. I don't like spiders either hahaha.

I won't show Derek your letters if you don't want me to, I promise, but I think he would find them interesting, like I do.

Best,
Jessica

P.S. I LOVE that picture you drew me. I think it's so cool how much you do with only ink and paper—is that all they let you have in there? But I could really see the cliffs and the waves and everything. And even though the girl you drew is prettier than me, I still think it's really nice, and I folded it up into a really small square so I can put it in my pocket and carry it everywhere.

January 15, 2001

Dear John,

Last night, Derek took me to a party. I told my mom I was
going to Caroline's to watch a movie and she was of course
so delighted at the idea of me having a friend to hang out
with that she didn't do much investigating.

The funny thing is when I met Derek I thought he was
the coolest guy on the planet earth, just because his hair is
long and he was wearing boots, and I'm so used to guys in
like basketball shorts or whatever. Actually I'm not used
to guys at all, that's possibly my whole problem. But when
we got to this party it was a whole room full of dudes that
looked like Derek. It was like something out of a weird
dream. There were only two other girls in the room. Right
after they told me their names I forgot. They were kind of
pretty, in a druggy way. I think they are like Maggie's age
or maybe a couple years older. You know how I said
teenage girls always have best friends? I could tell right
away that's what those two are, leaning into each other,
playing with each other's hair, like all the boys were just
extras in a movie about them. Looking at them made me
so lonely I wanted to die. I think Derek could tell because
he moved me so that I was sitting on his lap like a little kid.
And then he hushed everyone and said: "All right, boys
and girls. Here's a game for us to play. Who is your favorite
serial killer?"

The answers were pretty typical: Dahmer, Gacy, like three people said Richard Ramirez, and one dude said Fred and Rosemary West, who I actually hadn't heard of. The two girls argued over whether they would fuck Ted Bundy. I could tell all the guys were kind of into that conversation, and Derek could too, and so he was like, well, I have a surprise for you all, and then asked, in TV-host voice, "so, Miss Jessica, who is *your* favorite serial killer?" And of course, I said your name.

"And why is that, Miss Jessica?"

"Because we write letters to each other."

And all of a sudden there were a dozen eyes staring right at me, like I was a prophet. So I told them about Sara first, and how I started writing to you, and what you're like, how nice you are to me. I almost showed them the picture you drew for me, but I didn't, because it's too personal. I wanted to keep something for myself.

Derek and I kissed in his car, parked a block away from his house. I bit him, a little. He put his hand to his mouth to check for blood but there wasn't any. "You're like, feral," he said to me. Isn't that funny?

Jessica

February 1, 2001

Dear John,

The two girls from the party that Derek took me to are Lexi and Elaine. Derek gave Lexi my number and she called to ask if I wanted to come shopping with her and Elaine. I was surprised because they pretty much ignored me all that night. I should have known it was because they were watching me, the way girls do.

They came to pick me up. Elaine drove. My mom was at work and when I told Maggie I was going out with my friends she didn't even look up from her homework or her college applications or whatever she's up to lately. I could run away to join the circus and Maggie would not notice!

Lexi said to me: Elaine and I never like Derek's girl-friends, but we like you. He always goes for these googly-eyed girls, who look up at him like, ooooh, Derek, you're so smart.

"Bambi types," Elaine said. "But you seem cool. You seem like you have your shit together."

They asked how old I was and when I said almost sixteen they were surprised.

"You look younger," said Elaine. "But you act older."

"That's good," Lexi said. "Way, way better than the other way around."

They asked me a lot of questions about you, and also about Sara. They couldn't believe the guy who killed her never went to prison.

"Paul was in jail for like a month," Elaine told me. "For drug shit. I mean, it's just ridiculous."

"Fucking rich people," said Lexi.

"Lexi is a communist," explained Elaine. "Until she sees a lipstick she wants."

"Vive la revolution," Lexi said, and I couldn't help but think that if my mom or Maggie heard this conversation their heads would explode! Paul is one of Derek's friends. He doesn't seem like someone who has been to jail but I guess you never know with people.

Because Lexi said we were going shopping I thought she meant the mall but actually we went to a thrift shop. "Dead rich lady clothes," Lexi explained. "We find the best stuff here." She was right, there was a lot of cool stuff, a lot of real designer dresses and furs and things like that. Lexi and Elaine like to play a game where they choose the absolute ugliest stuff for the other one to wear. The lady behind the counter was not happy with us, I can tell you that, but she seemed to calm down when Lexi bought a pair of earrings, big silver hoops with little bells hanging off them.

When we were back in the car, Elaine said: I have a surprise for you. She opened up her bag and pulled out a dress, made of light blue satin, that I had been looking at in the store, running my fingers over it because it was so soft and shiny I couldn't believe it was real.

"You bought this for me?" I asked, like an idiot, and they both laughed, but nice laughing, not mean laughing as if I had made a very good joke.

"I knew I liked her," Elaine said to Lexi, like I wasn't even there. Anyway I don't know what to DO with the dress, because if I wear it anywhere my mom will demand to know where I got it. But it's so pretty. I'll try to get someone to take a picture of me in it and I'll send it to you.

Jessica

February 8, 2001

Dear Mr. Logan,

No Elaine and Lexi are not slutty! I don't know why you think that. Lexi and Paul have been together for I think TWO YEARS and Elaine is just very sweet and nice. It's not right for you to say that about them because you don't even know them. I thought you would be happy for me that I have friends and am having fun.

Sincerely,

Jessica

February 20, 2001

I accept your apology. You're right that Derek and all of them are older than me but I don't think they're trying to take advantage of me or anything. I guess the whole point is I wouldn't be able to tell if they were? But I'm not some dumb kid. I can look out for myself.

Funny news: Elaine is rich! I know this because she took us to her house. She seemed kind of embarrassed showing us around. Lexi must have been there before because she seemed totally comfortable, SO comfortable she picked an apple off the tree and ate it, just like that!

Bad news: My mom found one of your letters. It fell out of my backpack I guess? Actually I suspect she was snooping around but who knows. Anyway my mom was furious. I pointed out to her that it is my right as an AMERICAN to write to whoever I want and I thought she would hit me which she never ever has. My mom is a paralegal so she is big on civil liberties.

Then she asked me a lot of stupid questions. She said I have to see a psychiatrist. I think she expected me to put up a big fight but I think it might be kind of fun actually? It made me think of Silence of the Lambs which she doesn't even know that I've seen. Maggie was absent from this whole ordeal. When I told her about it she said something kind of mean like "maybe you can put therapy as an extracurricular on your college applications."

Anyway that is why this letter is a little late and also I postmarked it from the comic book store that's close to my school. You should probably mail stuff to me there from now on and they'll give it to me. I hang out there a lot anyway.

Sincerely,
Jessica

March 3, 2001

Dear John,

I see the therapist once a week now, after school on Wednesdays. She's a child psychologist so her office has lots of stuffed animals and dolls and I am not kidding you, a fucking dollhouse. It's insulting.

After my first appointment my mom sat down with me at the kitchen table to discuss it. I told her, you should be glad I'm doing this. Or at least relieved. There are kids my age who are doing drugs, drinking, having unprotected sex. Actually there are kids my age who are IN PRISON.

Derek's been weird to me lately, kind of cold, like he's sick of me. I asked Elaine about it and she said don't be paranoid. She said it in a nice way but she's been friends with him way longer than me so maybe she's lying.

I'll be sixteen on June fourth.

Sincerely,
Jessica

March 15, 2001

Dear John,

Today my mom drove me to therapy. As we were approaching Dr. Whelan's office she turned the music down and said, I looked him up. This fellow you've been writing to. She said: I went to the library and asked for help. They gave me everything they could find on him. I couldn't read it all, it made me sick. Jessica, honey, this is serious. This is real. It's not a fucking scary movie. It's REAL. Let me tell you my mom NEVER swears and it sort of unsettled me.

I said I know that. She said I don't think you do. If you did, you wouldn't be writing him letters. The things he did, honey, they are so bad. You can't even understand them. I don't think anyone can.

I wish I could explain to her: that's exactly why I'm writing to you! Because no one understands it but maybe I can. And if I can, wouldn't that be cool?

Best,
Jessica

March 26, 2001

Dear John,

Maggie told me she found brochures in mom's desk for Christian boarding schools. Those places are fucking serious, she told me. They lock you in dark rooms. They tell all the other kids not to talk to you and if they do they'll get punished.

I can't tell if she's trying to scare me or if she's for real. Anyway why should she care? She got into Bates with a big fat scholarship so now she's the Favorite Daughter forever and ever.

Anyway all those schools are run by evangelicals and despite being divorced my mom is super catholic and doesn't trust evangelicals. Though it would be typical of her to send me away RIGHT when I finally have friends. So I'm kind of scared but not that scared.

Sincerely,

Jessica

April 2, 2001

Derek took me to see Jeepers Creepers, which was nice, because we haven't been able to hang out that much lately, because he's been so busy with school. I kind of think he took me to see a horror movie as like a test, to see if it would scare me. It didn't. I didn't think it was that good but it definitely didn't scare me. After we went and got pizza. I could tell people were looking at us, looking at him especially, because this town I live in is so small and boring Derek seems like a rockstar in comparison to everyone else. It felt good.

I showed him the new drawing of the dogs that you sent me but none of your letters, I promise. I won't unless you say that I can.

Then we went to his house. His parents were upstairs watching TV and his sister was doing her homework. We went to the basement and I'm not stupid, I know what that means. I said we can fool around (isn't that the stupidest phrase? I HATE it) but I don't want to have sex yet. He was really nice about that. He even drove me home. The day after tomorrow his family is going on vacation to the Adirondacks for two weeks.

Best,
Jessica

April 10, 2001

I TOLD you I didn't show him any of your letters! I don't know why you don't believe me.

Jessica

April 23, 2001

Dear Mr. Logan,

Derek broke up with me. I've been crying like a little baby, crying so much I can't even sleep. It's so stupid because it's not like I even liked him that much! And I don't want Maggie or my mom to see me because then I have to explain why I'm so sad and then I'll be in huge trouble which is just what I need.

Even in school I just want to cry and I can't help it. I started crying in fucking HISTORY CLASS. I would be so embarrassed I could die except I don't give a shit about anyone at that fucking school. The nurse let me lie down in the sick room. I'm really worried that Maggie will hear about it and then I don't know what I will do.

Jessica

May 7, 2001

I know I'm not going to care forever. I know in like five years I'll think about Derek and Lexi and all of them and I won't care at all, I'll be like, what idiots. But right now I am so angry and sad I just want to SCREAM at everything and everyone. You're lucky I'm writing you letters otherwise I would want to scream at you too!

Thank you for the drawing by the way. It doesn't really look like him but it's funny and it made me laugh. And you were right about Lexi and Elaine. Not that they are sluts necessarily though who knows! But definitely they were not my friends. They are loyal to each other and to Derek but NOT to me.

When I called Lexi she pretended to give a shit for like ten minutes, saying things like Oh you're better off without him you're going to meet someone wonderful just you wait! It was like something a girl in a movie would say when the main character gets dumped but it was better than nothing and then all of a sudden she was like sorry got to go! And I haven't heard from her since. Elaine isn't even answering her fucking phone. It's like someone reached inside of me and turned off all the lights.

May 15, 2001

Dear John,

Last night was Elaine's birthday. I knew for a fact that she was having a party because she told me about it when Derek and I were still together. And it's not like I couldn't tell I was no longer invited, I'm not fucking stupid, but you know how I've been feeling lately, and the idea of all of them hanging out in Elaine's big beautiful house, having fun without me, it made me so crazy, I mean really crazy, like I was watching myself do stuff and thinking: Wow that girl is so dumb! She is going to get in so much trouble! I rode my bike to Elaine's house, like two hours away from mine. I snuck in through the back garden gate. I could see inside the living room, where they were all hanging out. Loud music and bare feet because of all the white carpets. Drinking something brown out of big glasses. They were watching a movie but not really, more talking to each other, laughing. There were cards on the floor like they were playing a game and got bored of it. All of them in that room, together, just being happy and normal, and it felt like they were standing in a circle taking turns stabbing me. Do you think I'm exaggerating? I know it's stupid but that's exactly how it felt. I thought I would cry but I couldn't.

Instead I had an idea that I would knock against the glass and hide, just to scare them a little. I thought maybe if I did it a few times it would really creep them out especially if they were watching a horror movie and already in kind of a scared mood. But the second my hand touched the glass a bunch of lights turned on in the garden and an alarm started blaring. I must have looked so stupid, so pathetic, just standing there. The only thing that makes me feel better is that I saw Derek's face and he was at least a little scared. I could tell.

The police came, and Elaine's parents, and then my mom. Elaine's parents aren't pressing charges (it's not like I did anything that bad, or hurt anyone, or was even trying to) but my mom has not said a word to me since she picked me up. Maggie tried to get me to talk to her but I don't feel like it. She's really going to send you away now, she said, but more like a warning than she was trying to rub it in. Except if mom's made up her mind there's not much point in warning me is there?

Maybe boarding school wouldn't be so bad? Especially if all the people there are there because no one wants to deal with them, maybe I could make some real friends. I'm trying to be optimistic, haha. Only thing is I don't think they'll let me write to you if I have to go there.

Best,

Jessica

Lizzie

In the week before her disappearance, Sara was working on an essay for her class on Giambattista Basile, the Italian folklorist. Her essay compared one of Basile's tales, "The Handless Princess," to the story of Saint Lucy. According to many versions of the story, Lucy, who had taken an oath of chastity, gouged out her eyes to dissuade a persistent suitor. When her own brother wished to marry her, Basile's virtuous, unlucky princess chopped off her hands.

Sara never finished the first draft. She had a tendency to procrastinate and would probably have completed the essay the same morning that it was due. In the margin of her notebook, she wrote: *should just cut off their dicks, instead.* Sara's notebooks, like her clothes, and her nail polish collection, and her camera, went to Lizzie after she died. Sara's parents distributed her belongings haphazardly after the police said that they would not be needed as evidence.

Five years after Sara's death, Lizzie sometimes wears her clothes, loose-fitting Levi's and flannel shirts with paint stains on the sleeves. She hopes that if she dresses like an artist, people might assume she is one. She lives in New York City now, with her fiancé, Leo. He went to the same college as Sara and Lizzie, but graduated a year before they started. Lizzie met him at an alumni Christmas party the winter after she graduated.

She never thought of herself as the kind of person who would go to alumni events, but that's how lonely she was, working as a receptionist in an Upper East Side retirement home, living in a tiny apartment that smelled like cat piss. In the months after Sara died, Lizzie's haze of grief and rage had kept her from making any real plans.

Lizzie used to hate New York. She hated the piles of trash along the sidewalk, she hated all the sirens, she hated the men who yelled obscenities at her on the subway, she hated the businessmen who stared at their watches and did nothing. In those first few years after Sara died, Lizzie did not just miss her friend, but envied her. Sara did not have to worry about health insurance or student loans or her career path. She would remain smart and beautiful forever without even trying.

It's not so bad anymore. She and Leo live in a small apartment near Morningside Park. He's in his last year of medical school at Columbia, studying to become a psychiatrist. Lizzie edits textbooks for a big publishing house downtown. Her cubicle is full of cacti in brightly painted bowls and postcards she bought in the MoMA gift store.

Last year, they adopted a dog, a big, goofy German shepherd named Annette. They got her because Lizzie often gets restless at night, but walking around alone makes her nervous. She loves the freedom that comes with having such a large animal by her side. It's how she imagines it feels to be a man.

It is a sunny Saturday in April. One of Leo's mentors has invited them to a dinner party. Leo asked if Lizzie wouldn't mind picking up flowers.

First, she has a hair appointment. Throughout college, Lizzie's hair was all sorts of colors: red, black, white-blonde, even turquoise. It's taken some effort to return it to the warm, pretty brown she was born with.

Margaret, her hairdresser, is a thin, austere woman who doesn't talk much. Across the salon, a customer is speaking to her own hairdresser quite loudly.

"I used to be an EMT," the woman is saying.

"Uh-huh. Wow. That must have been stressful."

"A little. But I never saw anything that bad. Not like on TV. Sometimes people had a little glass in their face, or a broken arm."

"What was the worst thing you saw?" the hairdresser asks.

"Oh. There was a girl who crashed her car into a guardrail, but she wasn't that injured. She was just sort of—stuck inside the car. She was wearing this gorgeous brown leather skirt. And she was so beautiful. I remember saying to her: You're so beautiful, and I'm so sorry this happened to you. Remember when leather pants and skirts were in fashion?"

Did you really say that? Lizzie wants to know. *Couldn't you get fired?*

She imagines the beautiful woman in the car, how confused and afraid she must have been, and there was this EMT, telling her how nice her skirt was. She probably thought it was a bad dream.

"Are you all right?" Margaret asks.

"I'm fine," Lizzie answers.

"Would you like some water?"

"Yes, please."

Several teenage girls walk past the salon, shopping bags dangling from their thin arms, wearing tank tops that make their shoulder blades look like angel wings.

Margaret gives Lizzie a paper cup full of water, which she gulps down gratefully.

"Any better?"

"Yes, of course. Thank you."

While she waits for her color to set, Lizzie flips through one of the women's magazines scattered around the salon. The actress on the cover has a face as delicate as a birdcage. Most of the pages are dedicated to diet tips and stilettos, but right in the middle there's an article called "How I Forgave My Daughter's Killer."

The title is in big red letters, printed above a photograph that looks like it belongs in a Christmas card or a high school yearbook. The girl in the picture is sixteen or seventeen, wearing a purple dress with a puffy skirt. A boy, around the same age, is standing beside her, his long arm draped over her bare shoulders. Both of them are grinning.

> The best day of my life was the day my daughter, Theresa, was born. The worst day of my life was when I learned that she was dead.

The author of the article describes her daughter in the same words that are always used for dead girls. *Beautiful, kind, generous, clever, sweet.* No one ever says: *She was a real piece of work*, or even, *She could be a brat sometimes*. At least some women who die tragically young must be something other than angelic.

From the first paragraph, Lizzie learns that Theresa was killed by her boyfriend. *What a surprise*, she thinks, numbly. She continues to read.

> Before Theresa was murdered, "forgiveness" was just a word to me. So was "faith." I believed in God, but I never heard His voice in my heart, because I never needed Him. Theresa, my angel, guided me to Him.
>
> I wrote many letters to Jeremy before I finally sent one. At first, I wrote that I hated him, and that I wished he would burn in hell for taking my daughter

from me. If not for Jesus, I would still be living with this rage and sorrow today.

One of Lizzie's old therapists had suggested that she write Blake Campbell a letter. "You don't have to send it," he reassured her. "The point is to clarify your own emotions. It's about you, not him, now."

"I will when I'm ready," Lizzie had promised him, lying. She had nothing to say to Blake, not even inside her own head. The only honest letter she could write would be a scream pinned to a page.

> When I first visited Jeremy in prison, my whole body was shaking. I didn't think I could look him in the eye. But I did, and what I saw was not the face of a killer, but that of a scared little boy. Part of me wanted to hug him and tell him everything would be all right. Part of me wanted to hit him, to hurt him, to make him feel the pain he had caused me. I nearly ran outside. But Jesus convinced me to stay.
>
> In the years since Theresa's death, I have gotten to know Jeremy. He is neither a child nor a monster. He is a bright young man with so much to offer this world. If he were free, he could join the army to protect our country. He could study to become a doctor and save lives. He could teach, he could be a firefighter. He could raise a family. He could serve his community, and God.

In prison, he is wasting his life. This is not what our family wants for him, and it's not what Jesus wants, either.

Lizzie flips the page. There is a picture of Theresa as a baby, held in the author's plump arms. There is another of Theresa as a child, dressed as Snow White, clutching a plastic pumpkin basket. The text below reads: *Happier times.*

Like a lot of the people she knew in college, Lizzie had an artistic temperament without the talent to match. She's growing out of it, or trying to. Sara was the real thing. She won prizes for her paintings. The younger students in the art program worshipped her. Even Lizzie, through her haze of love and envy, could see how talented she was.

The obvious question about anyone who dies young: *What would she have done if?* Would Sara have worked at an art gallery in New York? Taught English in China? Become a famous painter? Actually, if she had lived, she probably would have married Blake.

They became friends their freshman year, part of the same loose gaggle of smart, sweet girls. Sara had the face of a silent film star, the kind of face that had gone out of fashion but was still striking—soft cheeks and big dark eyes. Lizzie, with her henna-red hair and her runner's legs, was the one boys stared at when she entered the room, but it was Sara they wanted to talk to long after the party had ended. *She doesn't really care*, Lizzie always wanted to tell them, as Sara stared intently at the boy rambling about Truffaut or Trotsky or whatever the fuck they thought would impress her. *She doesn't give a shit about you or what you're saying, she just likes attention. She's making you feel interesting and important, because that's how she wants you to make her feel.* It almost always worked.

Sara had an aversion—was it actually an inability?—to saying no to anything, ever. When they first met, this intoxicated Lizzie. By the time they were seniors it exhausted her. It was because of Sara that Lizzie went to parties that she never would have been invited to otherwise. It was because Sara suggested it that Lizzie posed nude for life-drawing classes, which was thrilling, at least before it became tedious and embarrassing. Sara even cut Lizzie's hair short one dull evening. "You'll look just like Jean Seberg," she said. Lizzie did not. But the feeling of Sara's long fingers at her scalp made the haircut—which took years to grow out—almost worth it.

With Sara, Lizzie tried ecstasy, a glittering experience that left her aching and miserable for days after. She slept with boys she found unattractive and uninteresting, just so that she'd have something to talk to Sara about after. Lizzie even wrote some bad, short poems under Sara's influence.

Their junior year, Lizzie and Sara moved into a house off campus. It was tiny and perfect, painted yellow, with a small garden they tended to like old ladies.

Blake and Sara started dating that spring. They both knew him by name, even before he and Sara started hanging out, because he was so absurdly good-looking. More than once Lizzie had witnessed a girl at a party act like she had a head injury when Blake spoke to her. He asked Sara to dinner after seeing one of her paintings in a student art exhibition. On their first date, he brought her a bouquet of wildflowers tied with twine, and a weird little poem he wrote for her.

Shortly after Blake and Sara started dating, Sara woke Lizzie in the middle of the night, begging her for a ride to the hospital. Blake had some kind of accident, she'd said. It wasn't until days later that Lizzie found out what the accident really was—he had stuck a needle through his hand while trying to sew Sara's name into his palm. People at Crawford were always doing stupid shit and calling it art, and at first that's what Lizzie assumed it was. She also assumed Sara, who was too smart to fall for that kind of thing, would break up with Blake. But she didn't. In fact the whole disaster brought the two of them closer together.

Lizzie had no idea how to talk to Sara about it. She didn't want Sara to think that she was judging her. The whole thing made her wonder if Sara and Blake knew something about love that she didn't, that she was just too immature to understand. For many years, she was sick with guilt for not saying anything. It was Leo who finally reassured her.

"People who hurt themselves don't usually hurt others," he told her. "There's no way you or Sara or anyone could have known what would happen. And anyway, even if you'd had an idea, would she really have listened to you?"

Lizzie admitted that Sara probably wouldn't have. She and Blake lived in their own universe. Lizzie was not invited.

In the days before she disappeared, Sara was stressed about her senior thesis show. She didn't think it was her strongest work, and she was hard on herself. This is what Lizzie told the police. Personally, she believed Sara had run away—put herself on a bus to Chicago or maybe Montreal. She'd heard of Crawford students doing that. Lizzie was angry and lonely in their little house all by herself.

A local housewife found Sara, in a shallow grave of dirt and snow. Sara, who did not like scary movies, who spoke to cats and dogs as if they were people, who preferred to read the news because she found watching it on television overwhelming. All the life leaked out of her.

In the cab home from the salon, Lizzie tries, as she has tried so many times before, to imagine Sara's last moments: the knife, Blake's face, the sound of the water. The images are fleeting and far away, like watching a movie through the window of someone else's house. It is empty, empty, empty.

Whenever anyone talks about women who die young, they say how sad and terrible it is that these women never got a chance to have a real life, with a job and kids and marriage. But lots of women don't get to do those things, or don't want to. And Lizzie has a job, and she's about to get married, and she'll probably have kids at some point—but so what? *Who fucking cares?* she thinks, on the verge of tears. What exactly is Sara missing out on?

Lizzie puts the notebook back in its place. She goes into the bathroom and stands over the toilet, willing herself to vomit, but nothing happens. Then she crawls into bed with her clothes on and falls asleep.

In her dream, Lizzie is sitting in the passenger seat of a car. The woman from the article, the mother, is driving. She is saying something, talking too fast for Lizzie to understand. There is someone in the backseat. Lizzie can feel the person's presence, but she can't see who it is. She tries to turn her head, but she can't move it enough. Theresa's mother, who looks a lot like Lizzie's mother, is speaking loudly, but Lizzie still doesn't know what she's saying.

"Lizzie, wake up!"

Leo is towering over her. She puts a hand over her eyes to protect them from the light.

"Hello." Her skin is sticky with sweat, and the sheets have left a pattern on her cheek.

"What are you doing? We need to go."

"Shit. What time is it?"

"Quarter to eight."

"Oh, shit." She scrambles to her feet. "I'll get ready right now."

"I can't be late to this. It would look really bad."

I ask so little of you, he could say, but doesn't.

"I know, I know. I wasn't feeling well. I'm sorry."

"What kind of not well?"

"Nauseated. Kind of dizzy. But I'm fine."

"Did you take your meds today?"

"Yes."

"OK. I'll get you a glass of water. Get ready quickly, please. You can do your makeup in the car."

The dress she has chosen for the evening is made of dark green silk. It hits her right above her knees and is a little too tight around her waist. Lizzie stands in front of the mirror, hands on her hips, deciding whether or not to wear stockings.

She looks down at her body. There's nothing ugly or unusual about it—no scars or lumps or blemishes—but there is so *much* of it. Does she really need all this flesh, humming with blood?

Lizzie presses the palms of her hands against her thighs. She wants to jettison her extra flesh. Surely all women feel like this sometimes, whether or not their friends are dead.

"Lizzie? Sweetheart?" Leo knocks on the door and then opens it without waiting for her reply. "We need to go."

"I'm ready. Give me just one minute."

He hands her two aspirin and a glass of water, which she takes, dutifully.

"You look gorgeous," he tells her.

"I got my hair done."

"It looks great, Liz. We really need to go."

"I'm just putting on my shoes."

It is difficult for her to fasten the delicate straps around her ankles because her hands are shaking, but she manages. She's going to have to bring her body to dinner and leave her brain behind.

In the cab, she paints her lips pink. Leo fiddles with his cuff links. The cab halts at a light, and she lurches forward, dropping the tube of lipstick.

"Shit." She picks it up and inspects it for dirt. It's fine.

Lizzie examines her cheeks in the rearview mirror.

"I didn't bring any blush," she tells Leo. "Can you slap my face for me, please?"

He laughs and holds her left hand in both of his. "Make me this late again and maybe I will."

The cab moves to the side of the road to allow a stream of emergency vehicles to pass.

"Must be some kind of accident," Leo says, leaning over to look.

"I'm going to go around, yeah?" says the cab driver.

"Yes, that's fine," Leo answers.

Lizzie leans into him, catlike. This is how he likes her: sweet, and warm, easy to be around.

"You know," says Leo, staring out the window, "there are certain theoretical physicists who believe our universe is a hologram projected across a black hole."

"Really?"

"Well, it's not a widely held theory. But it would explain how gravity works."

"Do you think that?"

"It's not my field of expertise. I do think it's an interesting idea. And an appealing one. It sort of takes the pressure off, don't you think?"

"Yes, it does. I like that." She runs a thumb against the soft fabric of his sleeve.

"This looks good on you. You look good."

"Thanks, babe."

He is so handsome, Lizzie thinks. But it's more than that. He's a grown-up. He will lead her by the hand into the real world.

One night, shortly after she and Sara moved into their house, Lizzie awoke to find Sara beside her in bed, curled up like a seashell, facing the wall.

"What's going on? Are you OK?"

"Mhhm. Bad dream," said Sara, turning around and pressing her forehead to Lizzie's shoulder.

"What was it about?"

"I can't remember."

In the half-light, Sara's eyelashes looked like spiders' legs. She shifted, revealing white polka-dot underwear, frayed at the edges. There was a big bruise on her shin from dropping a box she was trying to carry upstairs.

"I'm sorry to wake you," she said softly. "I just want to be not alone for like, an hour. And then I'll be fine."

"It's all right," said Lizzie. She was already drifting out of consciousness. She could feel Sara's hair, like a soft animal, against her back. When she awoke again, it was morning, and she was alone.

Christabel

In his career as sheriff, Jonathan has dealt with all sorts of unpleasant people: petty criminals, meth addicts, plenty of drunk drivers, a woman who drowned her three-year-old in a bathtub. None of them ever unsettled him as thoroughly as Christabel Morgan, grief coming off her like a stench.

She is soft-spoken and courteous. She looks like any other small-town mom, just skinnier, and sadder. She is odd, but polite about her eccentricities, like refusing to drive at night, and washing her hands every hour. If she knows how nervous she makes people, it doesn't seem to bother her. Christabel lives in her own world. This one has little to offer her.

Every time she enters the sheriff's office—four times in the past six years—she looks around as if seeing it for the first time. Like the linoleum floors and corkboards covered in fliers are the streets of Paris, or the surface of the moon. You wouldn't know from looking at her that Christabel grew up here. She graduated from high school two years before Jonathan started. Unlike him, she left for college— Smith, where she studied anthropology, according to the bio on her website.

As far as websites for psychics go, Christabel's is relatively tasteful. It includes links to articles about cases she's helped solve, a few glowing client testimonials, and an online shop where you can purchase "highly charged amethyst geodes" for upward of seventy-five dollars.

They don't call Christabel unless the victim's family specifically asks for her. The first time she helped them was when Jacqueline Linder went missing. Jacqueline was very old, and her daughter was a regular client of Christabel's.

It was Christabel who told them where to find the body, in the middle of the woods behind Jacqueline's house. She had wandered off and froze to death. There was no sign of foul play. They would have found the body eventually, once the snow melted, but Christabel helped them speed up the process. She told the family that Jacqueline had not suffered, and they seemed to believe her.

The case in question today is that of William Stoddard, age nine, disappeared from his home two weeks ago. There was no sign of forced entry. The air-conditioning was broken and the family was sleeping with the windows open. Statistically speaking, William is dead, and it's just a question of how, and who is responsible.

The receptionist, Joyce, leads Christabel down the hall. Joyce is a real professional. She could be leading Christabel to her table at a fancy restaurant, or to her execution. Her face betrays nothing.

"Would either of you like some coffee?" she asks.

"Yes, please," says Jonathan. Christabel shakes her head.

Christabel doesn't look the way Jonathan originally pictured a professional medium. No silk scarves or dangling earrings. She dresses simply, black skirt and a white button-down top. She is very thin, her body pared down to almost nothing. All the bones in the back of her hand are visible.

Jonathan wonders how long it's been since she's had sex. She's not unattractive, but he doesn't even like shaking her hand.

Joyce comes in with the coffee and sets it on the table. Jonathan takes a deep breath, as if that might help steady his nerves.

"I assume you already know a bit about William Stoddard," he says.

"Yes. I've been reading about it. Those poor parents," Christabel says, which is what everyone says, even though she probably knows—as Jonathan does—that Henry Stoddard, an optometrist, and Rosalee Stoddard, a yoga instructor, are the people most likely responsible for their son's disappearance.

But maybe not.

"What do you know about the case?"

Christabel closes her eyes, like a child about to recite a poem. "That he's little. Six, seven?" *Is it painful for her to discuss this?* Jonathan wonders.

"Nine, actually."

"Oh. OK. I also know that he disappeared from his house, and that there are no suspects."

"That's it, pretty much."

"No suspects at all?"

"Nope." They questioned all the local creeps and sex offenders, but they all have alibis.

"Do you think he might have run away?"

"It's not impossible, but even if he had, a nine-year-old from this town, he wouldn't last that long. Either he would have chickened out and come back by now, or . . ." He allows himself to trail off.

Christabel shudders. "Poor kid. Poor family. I'm surprised it hasn't been a bigger story, you know, in the news."

"Well, a lot of parents, in these situations, they say yes to every interview, every TV show, just to get the word out. Sometimes it helps, sometimes not really. But the Stoddards are very private people. It's not their style."

"Do you find that suspicious?" she asks very lightly.

Jonathan shrugs. "Not necessarily. People behave all sorts of ways under stress, extreme stress. I try to just look at evidence. Analyzing behavior is someone else's job."

By "someone else" he means the state police, who have set up shop across the hall. He told them that Christabel was coming in today, and they showed little interest, probably dismissing her—who can blame them?—as small-town nonsense.

"I've never worked a missing child case before," she says. She is picking at the edges of her fingernails, which are painted a tasteful seashell pink. There are no rings on her fingers, no bracelets around her wrists.

"That's completely OK," he answers, a little annoyed at having to soothe her. "Anything you can give us, anything at all, might help." He's trying to say, *Just do your best*, but it comes out more like, *We are so desperate, we will take whatever you can offer.*

She gathers up her bag. It's a big leather satchel, like something a kid at a private school might be required to wear.

"Well, I'd like to go to William's house."

Six years ago, on a warm August night, a woman was attacked while jogging. A man hit her in the back of the head and dragged her into a wooded area, where he beat her, breaking one of her ribs. When she was found the next morning, neither her wallet nor her wedding ring had been taken, and she had not been raped. The man was never found, and a similar attack never recurred. Until now, Jonathan considered it his most disturbing case. Had the woman been robbed, or raped, or even killed, it would not have been so unsettling. Desire, no matter how perverse, was what made violence legible. Someone did this in order to get that. Without desire, without motive, the man might as well have been a ghost. No wonder they never found him.

It is the end of the summer. The lawn outside the Stoddard house is turning brown, and there are azaleas blooming all around, obscenely pink. Jonathan and Christabel arrive at eight, as the sky is just starting to get dark.

The Stoddards live in what used to be a farmhouse. It's big for three people, which makes Jonathan think they wanted more children. They moved up here from New York before William was born, probably to escape the terrors and temptations of the city. Inside, it's beautifully decorated, with thick, soft carpets and silver doorknobs. But it smells slightly off, like rotting fruit. On a table by the front door is a crystal vase full of nothing but dirty water.

Rosalee makes tea. It's too hot to drink, but Jonathan knows she needs something to do. A little terrier patters after her, forlorn. Jonathan hopes someone is remembering to feed it.

"How are you holding up?" Jonathan asks the Stoddards.

"Well, you know," Henry says. A stupid answer to a stupid question.

"It's a pleasure to meet you," Christabel says, sticking out her hand. Henry shakes it easily, as if they were strangers meeting at a cocktail party. But Rosalee clasps on to her.

"I'm so glad you're here. I did a lot of research, and everyone says you're the best."

Jonathan suspects this isn't exactly true. Most likely, it's that no one has called Christabel a charlatan, at least not online. He finds it interesting that there is no assumption of good faith among professional psychics. They're always accusing each other of being frauds.

"Thank you," says Christabel. She is not quite meeting Rosalee's stare. "I don't want to make any promises. But I will do whatever I can to help."

"I know. I know you will." Rosalee's voice is breathless. Jonathan is struck by how much she resembles a little girl, with her thin arms and her big watery eyes. "I know what happened to your poor daughter, and I know that you understand what we're going through. No one else does, but you do."

It's the first time Jonathan has ever heard someone mention Sara Morgan's murder to Christabel's face. Christabel doesn't react, she just continues to stare a few inches north of Rosalee's head. It's creepy.

"If it's all right with you, I'd like to look around the house. Just to get, you know, a sense."

Rosalee nods.

"I can show you around," Henry offers. "Give you the grand tour."

Like he's a fucking real estate agent. Some people are no good under stress, Jonathan knows. Some people collapse entirely. Some people just behave like their normal, gregarious selves, which is much weirder to watch.

Is it suspicious? It's no longer his job to wonder this, thank God, but if it was: *Yes, it's a little suspicious.*

"Thank you," answers Christabel. "But I'd rather do it myself. See where my instinct takes me."

"Sure," says Henry. "Whatever you want."

Police already combed the Stoddards' house, and their backyard, and the backyards of their neighbors, and the woods that lie just beyond the town. Nothing. The nearest body of water is a lake too big to drag properly, though they tried that, too.

Christabel disappears up a staircase. She walks very slowly, with a dancer's posture. They all watch her.

Jonathan wishes that he smoked, wishes that it were still socially acceptable, so that he could go outside instead of remaining in the Stoddard living room, which is starting to feel a bit like being buried alive. He checks his phone. There's a text from his pharmacy, reminding him to refill a prescription, and one from his wife, asking if he's OK with pot roast for dinner.

Jonathan's wife, Susanna, respects his work but would rather not know too much about it. He thinks that this suits him, too. She is a very sweet woman, a little more religious than he is, fond of dogs and swimming laps, which she does three times a week, her long light hair trapped in a cap that makes her look like an alien. They have raised two daughters to adulthood without incident, at least as far as he knows. Jonathan suspects this is the secret to being in law enforcement without losing your mind—decide which mysteries you should solve, and which ones you shouldn't.

When Jonathan was a child, his idol was his uncle Gary, a police officer. Gary was married to Jonathan's mother's sister, Helena. He was a big man, six foot five, passably handsome with a beard that mostly covered his acne scars. It wasn't that Jonathan lacked a father figure. His actual dad was a kind, moderately successful real estate agent whom he always considered a basically decent man. But it was Gary whom Jonathan worshipped. Gary himself coalesced with every cop Jonathan saw on television to create a living god, one who mostly ignored him but occasionally gave decent Christmas gifts.

After Jonathan entered the police academy, he and Gary started spending more time together, going out for beers, watching football. By that point Gary was the sheriff of his own small town, which was half an hour away from where Jonathan lived. It was incredible to be actual, grown-up friends with the man he had idolized as a child. He kept expecting the thrill to wear off, but it didn't. Every time their families gathered for a barbecue, it was like going to the Olympics.

In 2012 Gary and Helena got divorced. A couple of weeks later, Jonathan's mother called him in the middle of the night on the verge of tears. Helena was in her living room, half-hysterical, saying that Gary had held a gun to her head. Jonathan and Susanna drove over immediately. While Susanna tried to calm Helena, Jonathan discussed the situation with his mother.

"Do you think she's telling the truth?"

"Fucking Christ!" He had never heard his mother swear, and it made him nervous. "Do you think she would lie about something like this?"

"Not lie, no. But exaggerate? Maybe?"

"Exaggerate? Like, he only pointed the gun in her general direction?"

"Divorces can be messy," he said, helplessly.

To appease his mother, he stayed there that night. He slept on the couch, his father slept in the guest room, and Helena and his mother shared a bed. Susanna went home to be with their daughters and drove back in the morning to discuss what they should do next.

They sat around the kitchen table. Jonathan's father made eggs and sausages, though no one took more than a few bites.

"I can't get a restraining order," Helena said. "Those take forever."

"Maybe if you get a lawyer to help you?" suggested Jonathan's mother.

Helena shook her head. "Who will enforce it? All the guys in his department adore him. They'd do anything for him."

She wasn't wrong.

Jonathan suggested that Helena go to Minnesota and stay with her parents.

"How are they going to protect her? They're in their eighties," his mother snapped.

"He knows their address," Helena added. "We went there for Thanksgiving, twice."

It was too ludicrous, too gruesome, to think that Gary might follow his ex-wife to another state in order to harm her and her elderly parents. But it also wasn't that hard to imagine. Jonathan could already picture the headline: ESTRANGED HUSBAND MURDERS THREE. Not even a headline, he thought, more like a single sentence in some local paper. He had never thought of himself as a proud man, but the idea of his family reduced to tabloid cannon fodder, the worst kind of trash, made him sick with rage.

"I'll talk to him," he said. "I'll get to the bottom of it."

Of course, Gary denied it. They met at one of the bars they often frequented. It took two beers and shot of vodka for Jonathan to broach the subject. At first, Gary was outraged.

"I would never lay my hands on a woman. Any woman," he said. "You know that. Anyone who knows me knows that."

"I know," said Jonathan, idiotically. "I'm just trying to figure out what really happened, you know, why she would say that."

Gary shrugged. He seemed to have calmed down quite quickly. "Who knows. Maybe she saw it in a movie or something, got it mixed up with real life."

When Jonathan repeated this explanation to Susanna, later, she shouted with laughter.

"Saw it in a movie? What does he think, that she's four years old?"

He didn't want to admit that, at the time, it had sounded like a plausible explanation. That he had been relieved—see, no big deal, just an argument between exes, happens all the time. Susanna gripped his hands in hers and said sternly: "There are two options. Either Helena is lying, or he is. They can't both be telling the truth. You need to pick a side."

"I hate this," he told her.

"Yes," she said, gently. "It is terrible for you. But it's much worse for Helena."

It was Susanna's idea that Helena should stay with them. She would look after the kids, even though their daughters were too old to need a babysitter. Helena did her best to make herself useful. Their house was never as tidy, their garden never as abundant, as when she was there. She also accompanied their youngest daughter, Beth, as she practiced for her driving test.

Gary was fired after showing up to work drunk, twice. No pension, nothing. Jonathan felt sorry for him, but kept that to himself. Once he was no longer a police officer, Helena was a little less afraid of her ex-husband and, with Susanna's help, found a job as a live-in caretaker for an elderly woman. Jonathan didn't point out that if Gary really wanted to kill her, no longer having a government-issue weapon probably wouldn't stop him.

If not for Gary's fall from grace, Jonathan might still envision himself as the hero of this story, the good-hearted, sharp-eyed small-town sheriff who brings the innocent child safely home. Instead, he's just trying not to be the villain: the bumbling, arrogant small-town sheriff who lets the innocent child die and the murderer get away. When the state police came in, the lead investigator thanked Jonathan for being so cooperative. It felt like an insult. *Good for you, for realizing how useless you are. Thanks for not punishing the rest of us with your incompetence.*

The tea is lukewarm and tastes like dirt. It is unendurable, sitting here with these people, who are either the most depraved criminals he's ever met or the most tragic victims, just sitting across from him like they're watching a mildly interesting tennis match.

"I'm going to check on her," he says, and goes upstairs.

The staircase is narrow and rickety, and would probably be remodeled at some point, given different circumstances.

He can imagine a little William, learning to walk, being overwhelmed by the thin wooden steps.

William's room is the first door on the left. Jonathan remembers the day he was reported missing, instructing the Stoddards not to touch anything, anything could be evidence. He stood in this same doorway, watching the crime scene techs label every juice stain and mismatched sock. Since then the room has been tidied, William's clothes and toys put back in their place, his bed with its Mickey Mouse sheets neatly made. No child's room is this neat. It's like some kind of macabre museum.

Down the hall is Henry and Rosalee's room. One of them—he suspects Rosalee—has expensive tastes. There are candles in glass jars on top of the bureau and on the matching dark wood tables at each side of the bed. On the wall is a big mirror in a gold filigree frame, and the quilt on the bed is made of spotless white silk. This room is messier, clothes on the bed and floor, drawers left open. He sees food wrappers on the floor near the dustbin, like someone meant to throw them away but didn't quite make it. The laundry hamper in the closet is overflowing.

As Jonathan moves closer, he sees a pair of Rosalee's underwear, made of cream-colored lace, with a russet stain on the crotch. He notices the window has been left open. This makes him think that the Stoddards are not afraid. Either because what they cherish most has already been taken, or because they know, already, what has happened to him. Not his job, he has to remind himself.

"Christabel?" There is no response. He goes to the window, which overlooks the backyard. Christabel is there, sitting on the playset. She must have gone downstairs while he was focused on the underwear.

She is on the swings, her feet brushing the grass beneath. Unlike the Stoddard house, the playset is prefab and perfect, probably ordered from a catalog. There's a ladder and monkey bars and a tiny house, all made of shiny red and blue plastic. His kids would have loved something like this. Does it make Christabel think of her own daughter? And if it does, how can she stand it?

"Hey there," he says. He wants to sit on the swing next to her, but he's afraid his weight might bring the whole structure tumbling down.

She says nothing. She's swaying back and forth, dirt gathering on her white sneakers.

"Do you want to take a break?"

It's a stupid question—as if there is anywhere Christabel can go where she won't suffer—but she seems to appreciate him asking.

"I'm all right."

"Have you found anything?" he asks.

"Nothing," she says. "Most of these old places, there's something. Some murmurs. If a house has been around long enough, at least *one* person has died in it. I don't mean in a bad way, a violent way. People just used to die at home more, not in hospitals. Most of the time, I can sense that. But here, nothing. It's like it's been bleached clean."

"Jesus. What do you think that means?"

"I have no idea."

She is lying. Jonathan knows nothing about psychics, but he can recognize a lie when he sees one, especially one this obvious. Christabel knows what happened here, or thinks she does, and she is not telling him.

She looks more like a ghost than ever, swaying back and forth. He wants to grab her, to still her. He wants to scream, *Tell me what happened to that boy*, right in her strange white face.

He tells himself to relax. He has never believed in this psychic bullshit, and right now is a stupid time to start. Christabel doesn't know any more than he does. She's not supernatural, she's just creepy and sad, and the sooner they get out of there, the better.

"We can leave at any time. I'll drive you home," he says.

"That's nice of you."

She continues to sway until he puts a hand on the swing, steadying her. Then she stands up easily, obediently.

"Go wait by the car," he tells her. "I'll say good-bye to the Stoddards."

Christabel gives him her address, and he plugs it in the GPS. He turns on the radio so that it won't be so awkward for them to sit in silence, but it doesn't make him any less uncomfortable. He can't shake the certainty he felt at the Stoddards' house—that Christabel knows something and is choosing not to tell him.

Why not? The answer comes as easily as the idea: she wants to protect him. Whatever happened is so horrible that she doesn't want to burden anyone else with it. She's locking it inside herself for safekeeping.

He turns down the street toward a block of beige apartment buildings. The thin iron balconies are decorated with laundry and dead flowers in terra-cotta bowls. He wonders which one belongs to her.

"This is me," she says, cheerfully, undoing her seatbelt. "Thanks for the ride."

"No problem," he says.

"Would you like to come up for some tea?" she asks.

It seems impossibly rude to refuse.

He isn't sure what he expected. Lots of scarves, probably, and candles, and crystals, and shit like that. But Christabel's apartment looks like she ordered every item in it from one page of a catalog. The couch, the carpet, and the curtains are the same shade of grayish blue. On the coffee table is a pristine white orchid in full bloom. He can't quite figure out what the apartment smells like. Something slightly chemical, but not unpleasantly so, maybe some kind of cleaning liquid. The whole place is pristine.

"What kind of tea would you like?" Christabel asks.

"Anything without caffeine?"

"Smart," she says. "Have you ever had dandelion tea?"

"No," he admits. "I didn't know that existed."

"It's very good for you. Would you like to try some?"

"Sure. Thank you."

He sits on the couch. There's nothing there for him to busy himself with, no magazines or coffee-table books.

"May I use your restroom?" he asks.

"Sure. First door on the right."

The bathroom, too, is mostly blue, with blue tiles on the floor, and a blue-and-white-striped shower curtain. He can't resist the urge to check her medicine cabinet. It's mostly empty, except for a bottle of aspirin, some bobby pins, a tube of organic toothpaste, and Band-Aids. No prescription pills, he notes, though maybe she keeps those elsewhere. He returns to the living room. There are two frames on the wall. One is a picture of a pretty dark-haired girl who he assumes is Christabel's daughter. The other is a piece of paper with writing in scraggly letters. It takes him a minute to decipher what they say.

> The forest
> The forest
> Light leaking through the trees
> Moon sliced in two

Jonathan feels ashamed, but powerful, as if he were looking through Christabel's emails or watching her undress. He goes back to the couch. A cup of tea in a blue ceramic mug is waiting for him on the table. He's surprised by the taste, rich and sweet.

"This is really good," he says.

"I'm glad you like it. It's really good for your immune system."

They sit silently.

"You must really like the color blue," he notes.

"Yes," she smiles. "My favorite, since I was a kid. The benefits of living alone. You can have exactly what you want."

"It's a beautiful place. Very peaceful."

"Thank you. That's what I was going for."

"Well, you did a great job," he says, and then, because he can no longer stop himself:

"Do you miss her? Your daughter?"

She smiles at him with her eyes closed. "Why would I miss her? I speak to her every single day."

It's dark by the time he gets home. The neighbor's dog barks at him as he fiddles with his keys and unlocks the door.

The light in the kitchen is on. His eldest daughter is in North Carolina, at a beach house owned by her boyfriend's parents. His youngest, Beth, sits at the kitchen table on her laptop. He kisses her forehead, resisting the temptation to look at whatever's on her screen.

"How was your day?" she asks him.

"Not bad. Yours?"

"Not bad either. Mom and I went to the pool. She's so *fast*, I had no idea."

"Where is she now?"

"Upstairs, taking a shower. There's a plate of food for you in the fridge. We had pot roast. They're not that good."

"Thanks for the warning."

She waits for him to finish washing his hands at the kitchen sink.

"Have you found that little boy?"

There is no judgment in her voice, just curiosity, concern. Still, he doesn't want to meet her eyes.

"Not yet, honey."

She gives a sad, small smile, like she wants to say something encouraging, but knows better.

"I'm going to say hi to your mom," he tells her.

"OK, Dad. I'm probably going to bed pretty soon."

"Good night, then."

"Good night."

Upstairs, Susanna is in bed, folding down the corners of a magazine. She smells vaguely of chlorine, and of the lavender shower gel she uses, and of his cologne, which she claims to prefer to perfume. She's wearing a big Case Western T-shirt and a pair of lacy underwear, now more holes than fabric. She grins as he enters.

"How was your day?"

He flops on the bed, face-first, his shoes still on. She strokes the back of his head absently.

"That bad?"

"Not bad. Bizarre. Do you know—or remember— Christabel Morgan? Christabel Heller, when she grew up here."

"It sounds vaguely familiar, but no, I don't."

"Well, she's a psychic now."

"Oh, Christ." Susanna is even more skeptical of these things than he is.

"I know, I know. We don't let them anywhere near cases unless we're desperate, which we are. The interesting thing about her"—"interesting" was absolutely the wrong word, but he didn't know where to begin looking for a better one—"is that her daughter was murdered. And I'm not totally sure, but I think that's when she became a psychic."

"Spooky," said Susanna, and then, more seriously, "God, to lose a child. And like that. I can't imagine anything worse. I really can't. No wonder she lost it."

"That's the thing. I don't think she lost it. I don't think she can see the future in tea leaves, or anything like that. But if anyone had access to the shit the rest of us can't see, I think it would be her."

Under other circumstances, Susanna might have teased him for this, but instead she says: "I guess that's not impossible. That poor woman."

"But she's not . . ." Jonathan shrugs. "She's not grieving. And I don't mean she's moved through her loss or whatever. She said she speaks to her daughter every single day."

"Well. Maybe she does. Or thinks that she does. Maybe at some point there's no real difference."

They sit together in silence. He lets Susanna's hair run through his fingers like water.

"So, did she help you?"

"Sorry?"

"With the case."

"No. Not really." Without looking at her, he says, "I think she knows something, or thinks that she does, and she isn't telling me."

"That's so weird. What makes you think that?"

"Just a sense."

"Why would she lie to you?"

"Not lie, exactly. More like, keep something hidden that she doesn't want me to know. Like she's protecting someone."

"Who?"

"Fuck if I know. It's not her job to decide who gets protected, who gets to know what."

He can hear the anger and exhaustion in his voice. Susanna looks at him cautiously.

"You said she was a little kooky. Maybe she doesn't know anything anyway."

"No, probably not. You're right." He gets up and stretches. "Do you want some tea?"

"Chamomile, if we have any left. Thank you."

He goes downstairs to the kitchen. His daughter is still there, focusing hard on something in the darkness. The light from her laptop glows against her gold hair.

Luna

Fate would be a good excuse for what I did. I had graduated from college a month before, and I had no job prospects. Blake and Katherine Campbell needed a nanny for their five-year-old daughter, Ruby, and I had extensive child-care experience. It was a lucky break.

Except that I checked the social media accounts of both Blake and his wife nearly daily. His wife's interested me more. She posted beautiful photographs of her little girl, her blooming garden, the delicious meals she made using ingredients from both the garden and the health food store empire owned by Blake's parents. She had over five thousand followers on Instagram, mostly other environmentally conscious mothers like herself.

Blake posted pictures of his wife and daughter, and of the hikes they went on as a family, and of his band, the

Bad Teeth. Either he hadn't figured out the privacy settings on his Facebook, or he didn't care about them. I knew about the books he read (mostly memoirs by comedians) and the organizations he raised money for (mostly food banks and animal shelters). I knew what his band sounded like (folky, and not very good) and the details of his résumé (managing health food stores and occasional volunteer work).

At first his online openness shocked me. But I realized he had no reason to think anyone was looking for him, watching him. It had been fifteen years since he killed my half sister. She was now just a name on a plaque in a community garden, and he was a grown man with a job and a wife and a child. Not guilty, not guilty, not guilty. Sixty days in a mental hospital, a stint in rehab, and now he was back to being a real person.

I learned from Katherine's Instagram that the three of them were moving to Massachusetts and needed a nanny. Blake's father was opening a new health food store, which Blake would manage.

I sent Katherine an email. I put my mother's last name, rather than my father's, on my résumé. Three days later I got a response from Katherine. My heart skidded still at the sight of her name in my inbox. She asked if I could provide any references. The woman who ran the nursery school where I had worked part-time in college sent one. Katherine called and asked if I could come to their house to meet her and Ruby.

It was no problem, I said, and drove three hours to their house.

Their new house was vaguely Victorian-looking. I could imagine a real estate agent convincing them that it was elegant rather than creepy. Katherine greeted me at the door. She was taller than I expected. Her reddish hair was tied up in a messy bun. A golden retriever accompanied her, trying to lick my face. "Easy, Flower," she said to the dog, grabbing it by the collar.

"It's fine," I told her. "I like dogs."

"We're trying to teach her not to jump on people, but maybe that ship has sailed."

I pet the dog's head cautiously. I wanted to show that I was, in fact, fond of dogs, but I didn't want her to think I would encourage bad behavior.

"What did you say her name was?"

"Flower," she said, rolling her eyes. "That's what happens when you let a two-year-old name a dog."

"I think it's cute."

"I think so, too," she said, and laughed. "Come on in."

She wore a black linen dress and no shoes. Her legs were not shaved. She apologized for the boxes spread out across the floor of the living room. The dining room was cordoned off with plastic and tape while a crew of men painted it a pretty bluish green. I waved at them awkwardly.

Katherine took me upstairs. Flower trotted after us, whining quietly. Though the steps creaked, there was something very appealing, I had to admit, about a spiral staircase. *Good bones*, I imagined the real estate agent telling them.

First, she showed me Ruby's room. The walls were white, painted with animals: lions, tigers, pandas, cows, cats, chickens, and polar bears. I wondered who had painted them. They didn't quite look professionally done. There was a rocking chair by the window. Katherine gestured toward it.

"Ruby likes to be rocked before she goes to sleep, and that's usually when we read to her." There was a white wooden bookshelf in the shape of a dollhouse. I recognized some of the books I had liked as a child. Ruby's bed was made of white wood, with a pink-and-white-striped coverlet. At least a dozen dolls and stuffed animals were arranged neatly by the pillows.

"She loves dolls. We tried to raise her sort of, you know, gender-neutral. We bought her a plastic tool kit. She dumped all the tools out and wore it as a purse. What can you do? Her dress-up kit is over there, that little trunk by the bed. You might be subjected to some royal tea parties. I hope that's OK."

"That's great. Imaginative play is so important for kids."

Katherine raised her eyebrows at me, and then smiled.

"I agree, actually. My husband wants her to spend all day running around in the sun, but that's not the kind of child she is. She'd much rather be putting on a play, doing some kind of art project, that kind of stuff."

It was the first time she mentioned Blake. I felt a dull pressure at the back of my skull, but I continued to nod politely. She led me to a slightly smaller room next to Ruby's.

"This one would be yours, if you decide to come work for us. You can decorate it however you want, of course. Only downside is you have to share a bathroom with Ruby."

"I'm sure I'll survive," I said, brightly. I wanted to sound as cheerful and amenable as possible without revealing how desperately I wanted the job. *If you decide to come work for us*, she had said, as if she had already made up her mind to hire me, but I wasn't sure.

"My husband and I sleep down there," she said, pointing to a closed door at the end of a narrow hallway. "Let's go back downstairs."

She showed me around the kitchen, living room, dining room, and playroom. "Everything's a mess right now, but it'll all come together soon. We won't be living in chaos for much longer, I promise."

"I'm sure it'll be gorgeous when it's done," I said, and then kicked myself for being so obsequious. I felt the pressure in my skull again. But Katherine smiled at me. Maybe she was convinced.

"And here's the backyard," she said, leading me outside. "This is really what convinced us to buy this house. I'm sure you'll see why."

It was an expanse of perfect green, interrupted by only a few trees. Katherine led me to the end of the—field? It was far too big to be called a lawn—where there was a thin brook.

"The water is so clean, you can drink from it. Here, try."

She cupped her hands and filled them with water, and held them to my face. I drank, obediently.

"Wow," I said. "It's like a children's story." It actually was.

"I get nervous about all these rocks, of course," she said. "It's not quite deep enough to swim in, but you can certainly wade around. Ruby likes that."

"Where is she?" I asked.

"Playdate. She'll be home soon. I thought the two of you could play together for a little bit while I do some gardening, see how you get along. Does that sound good?"

"That's perfect."

She led me back inside. We drank green tea out of big white mugs, sitting on the back porch. "We'll have nice wicker chairs out here soon, I promise," she told me.

"Don't worry about it," I said. Was she trying to impress me? I told her about what I'd studied in college, and about working at the nursery school.

She asked about my parents. I answered carefully. My father, I told her, was a research scientist. I didn't really understand his work, but it had something to do with diabetes. My mother had been a lawyer, and then a stay-at-home-mom, and now she was considering going back to work. Katherine nodded and didn't ask any further questions. She wasn't interrogating me, of course. She just wanted to know that I came from a nice family.

We heard a car pull up in the driveway.

"That must be our girl," she said, standing up. The way she said *our girl* tugged at something in my brain. "You can just put your mug in the sink. I'll deal with it later."

A woman, presumably the mother of Ruby's playdate, brought her to the front door. She and Katherine spoke as Flower covered Ruby in kisses. Ruby's hair was almost the same color as Flower's fur. It was hard to tell where the girl ended and the dog began. I stood off to the side, like an idiot.

"Oh!" said Katherine. "Amy, this is Luna. Luna, Amy." The woman and I shook hands.

"I better get going," she said. "Ruby was an angel, as always. I'll see you around!"

Katherine closed the door behind her.

"Ruby," she said. "Can you say hi to Luna?"

Ruby gazed up at me. Her eyes were surprisingly dark. "Hi," she said.

"Stand up, please. Be polite."

Ruby stood up. She was wearing shorts and a T-shirt with a sequined butterfly. "Hi," she said again, more warily.

"Luna's going to play with you while Mommy does some work. Is that OK?"

Ruby nodded.

"Why don't you show Luna some of your books and toys?"

"OK," said Ruby. She had a funny, solemn way of talking. "I will show you where they live," she said to me. I allowed her to hold my hand as she led me up the spiral staircase. Children love to feel that they are in charge. I turned around to look at Katherine, who winked and gave me a thumbs-up.

"This is Elizabeth," said Ruby, holding up the biggest of her dolls.

"Is Elizabeth your favorite?" I asked.

"No, but she's the oldest."

We went through all the toys on her bed. They each had names.

"This is Billy," she said, pointing to a teddy bear. He was the most worn of all the toys. "My dad used to be Billy's father, but then he gave him to me, so now I'm his father."

I couldn't help but laugh at that. It was so sweet. But I didn't want Ruby to think I was laughing at her, so I said: "Wow! May I hold him?"

She considered for a moment. "No. But you can hold Moon Cat."

I held Moon Cat. This went on for about an hour.

"Ruby! Luna!" Katherine called from downstairs.

"It is probably time for dinner," Ruby explained generously.

"Maybe!" I said. "Let's go find out."

Katherine was at the kitchen table, slicing cucumbers into delicate circles. A tall man with a beard and very pale blue eyes was sitting next to her.

"Luna, this is my husband, Blake."

He stood up to shake my hand.

"Pleased to meet you," he said.

"Nice to meet you, too." The sharpness in my throat spread through my body. Even my toes hurt.

"How did it go?" Katherine asked.

"Really well, I thought," I said, looking at Ruby for confirmation. "Got to meet some new friends. Moon Cat and Billy and the whole crew."

Both Katherine and Blake laughed at that. Ruby moved toward her father, who put her on his lap. He was handsome enough that I would have noticed him if I'd walked past him on the street. Next to him Katherine looked ordinary and a little old. I wondered if she knew that.

"Would you like to join us for dinner?" he asked.

"I actually need to get going," I said. "But thank you so much. It was wonderful to meet all of you."

"I'll walk you out," Katherine said.

"Thank you so much," I repeated as we approached the front door.

"No, thank you. I think Ruby likes you a lot. I'll be in touch this week. If you don't hear from me, call, because I've probably just forgot."

"OK."

"I'm so glad you came by." She hugged me, which surprised me. She smelled of pine and wax and cleaning fluid.

"I'm glad, too."

I got into my car and drove for a few minutes, until I was sure I was completely out of sight of the house. Then I pulled over and laid my head on the steering wheel, expecting to cry.

I hate Blake much more than I loved Sara. I have no actual memories of Sara, because she died when I was two years old. I know her only as the bottomless hole of sadness she left in my father's life.

My third-grade circle of friends included a girl who had been adopted from Estonia. Once, at a sleepover, someone asked her how she found out that she was adopted, probably imagining some kind of dramatic scene. But the girl just shrugged and said, "I didn't find out. I never didn't know." It was like that with Sara. I just knew that I had a half sister and that she was killed by her boyfriend, the same way I knew my own name.

We didn't speak about her often. It's not that the subject was forbidden, but that there was very little to say. Sara and my mother were not close. From what my mother says, I suppose they were as friendly as a woman can be with her teenage stepdaughter. She said nice things about Sara, but they were generic. It's not that I doubted that she was, in fact, nice and pretty and talented, but what else could my mother have said? It was possible that she didn't want to speak ill of the dead, but it was also possible that Sara died before she got a chance to develop a real personality.

Sometimes a movie would come on television, and my father would say, "Sara loved this movie," or he might point out Sara's favorite kind of flower. As a teenager, I came to suspect that Sara did not really love *Some Like It Hot*, or white tulips, but that my father wanted an excuse to say her name, to impart some information about her to me, even if it was silly or false.

I never gave much thought to Blake until I was in ninth grade, when I was required to participate in a debate about the death penalty. I was assigned the "pro" side. I was never a great student, but the subject piqued my morbid curiosity, and I spent hours in the library researching Ted Bundy, Jeffrey Dahmer, John Wayne Gacy. My strategy was to find out as much as I could about the worst people we had ever heard of, in order to say to my classmates: *Do you really want these men to stay alive?* My opponents' arguments about human rights and due process paled in comparison to our stories of boys under floorboards. My teacher was less impressed and gave me a B.

I'm not actually in favor of the death penalty, I don't think. But reading about it made me wonder about the man who killed Sara. All I knew was that he was her boyfriend, that he was insane, and that he didn't go to prison. I wondered if that was because someone else might have done it, but my mother told me no, that he had confessed. She had been at the sentencing, to support my father. They left me at home with a babysitter.

"If he definitely did it, why didn't he go to jail?"

"They can't send you to jail if you're not sane. That's the law." My mother, a former lawyer, usually loved any opportunity to explain legal concepts to me, but this particular subject made her uncomfortable.

"So he just got to go home? That doesn't seem fair."

"I guess not. But that's how it works sometimes."

"Isn't dad angry about that?" I was thinking about a video I'd seen, the father of one of Bundy's victims, talking about what a relief it was when he was finally executed. But the father spoke like he was chewing glass.

"Your father forgave him," my mother said.

"Why?"

"You'll have to ask him that," she answered, knowing, I'm sure, that I wouldn't.

All teenagers grapple with the realization that the world is unjust. But for me this revelation was deeply personal, and it made me behave in bizarre ways. Some teenage girls torment their fathers by wearing short skirts or piercing their tongues. I asked mine questions about his dead daughter. He never answered them to my satisfaction, maybe because he couldn't.

I got my shit together once I went to college. Partly because I found a therapist I liked, and partly because I became addicted to following Blake online. If I were a more mystical person, I might say this: because he killed Sara, he now possessed her, and tracking the minutiae of his life was how I connected to her. But it might also just be the same ugly curiosity that kept me in the library until midnight, watching interviews with serial killers.

For what it's worth, I was a great nanny. Ruby wasn't always an easy kid, prone to temper tantrums and crying when kids at the park didn't want to play with her. She had an unusually loud voice for a kid her age, and I often had the impulse to cover her mouth with my hand, just to get a moment of peace. But I was good with her, patient but firm, and she got quite attached to me. Five is a weird age, developmentally, and I wonder if she'll remember me when she gets older.

I worked for the Campbells from the end of May to the beginning of August. In that time I sort of lost track of why I was there, not that I had any great clarity of purpose to begin with. My parents are big believers in the power of routine, and it pained me a little to admit that they were right. I was on my feet all day with Ruby, which meant I slept better at night than I had since I was a child. Because my week was so busy, I really savored Thursdays, which were my days off. I usually spent them sitting on a towel in the backyard, reading, or just staring at the sky and the trees. It was, overall, a pretty happy time in my life, which might be why I got careless.

I brought very little with me to the Campbells, just jeans and T-shirts and underwear, a toothbrush and toothpaste and a hairbrush. All my jewelry, all my makeup, my watch, my journal, my nice clothes—I left behind. The one sentimental object I took with me was a handsome hardbound copy of *Jane Eyre*. It was a gift from one of the women I worked with at the nursery school. My full name written on the inside cover.

Katherine was always busy. She sewed heart-shaped bags of muslin filled with dried flowers, which she sold online and in their store. She cooked almost everything from scratch, often using things they grew in their garden. She took an adult beginners ballet class on Wednesdays. All Ruby had to do was mention milkshakes, and Katherine would be at the kitchen counter, making whipped cream by hand.

But she didn't seem to take pleasure in any of it. She always looked tired to me, but maybe that was just her face. I wondered if she worked so hard to seem like an earth goddess because Blake was more beautiful than she was, because she felt that she needed to earn her place in the lovely world they inhabited.

I wondered what Ruby would look like when she got older, which of her parents she would resemble more. She was at an age where it was difficult not to be cute, but maybe someday her golden hair would darken, her rosy cheeks turn ruddy. I could easily imagine her as the same kind of chubby, sullen teenager that I was. Would Katherine have a hard time loving a child who wasn't beautiful? I suspected I would, which troubled me deeply.

One day, I took Ruby to Little Fairy World, a Disneyland knockoff thirty minutes from the Campbells' house. I found that place, with all its off-brand princesses and puppet shows, extremely depressing, but Ruby loved it. Katherine suggested that I take her there because the house would be full of construction workers all day. When it was time to leave, I found that my car battery was dead. I had Ruby sit in a shaded area of the parking lot while I tried to call Katherine, but she didn't answer her cell phone or her landline. Ruby was starting to melt down. I bought her another shaved ice and called Blake. While we waited for him to arrive, we watched one more puppet show and went on the Jolly Trolley, but neither of us enjoyed it. It was too hot, and Ruby needed a nap. Silently I begged her not to start crying.

When Blake showed up, he was wearing a suit.

"I'm so sorry," I said. "Did I interrupt something important?"

He waved me off. "It happens. Don't worry. Hi, Ruby. Did you have a fun day?"

She nodded, staring up at him adoringly. He picked her up in his arms. "She loves this place."

"I can tell," I said.

I held Ruby while he jumped my car. She had calmed down now that her father was near, and I felt her fall asleep against my shoulder. When the car was ready, Blake turned on the air-conditioning for a few minutes. Once it was cool enough, he put her in her car seat and kissed her forehead. She shifted slightly but did not wake up.

"Thanks," I said, quietly.

"Not a problem."

"Are you headed back to the house?" I asked him. I'd almost said *our house*.

"Got to finish up some things at work," he answered. "But I should be home for dinner. Will you tell Katie for me?"

"Of course."

"Great. Drive safely."

We stood there for a moment. I thought he might hug me. Eventually he shook my hand, which I thought was hilarious. Then we both drove our separate ways.

Jane Eyre resonated with me much more than it had in high school. I was enjoying it a lot, actually. One day, I left it out in the backyard, and Blake brought it inside to save it from an unexpected rainstorm. That's how he caught me.

He knocked on my door early in the morning. I quickly pulled on shorts and a T-shirt to answer.

"Hi there, Luna. Can we talk?"

I was suddenly aware of my lack of a bra.

"Uh, sure. What's up?"

"Why don't you get dressed and meet me downstairs," he said.

His tone frightened me. But it was a maybe-I'm-in-trouble kind of fear, not a maybe-he'll-kill-me kind of fear. I did what he said.

"Let's go for a walk," he said, when I met him in the kitchen.

In the backyard, violets and dandelions and moon daisies pushed up through the grass, which was still wet from rain. Katherine's rosebushes hummed with the activity of insects. The leaves of the trees, almost obscenely green, rustled like silk skirts. It occurred to me that I was in a truly dangerous situation.

"I'm not going into the woods with you," I said.

"We don't have to," he answered. "I just thought we should talk privately."

"This is private enough," I said.

He raised his eyebrows.

"OK, Luna."

The way he said my name, I knew that he knew. He sighed deeply and handed me the copy of *Jane Eyre*. I held it tightly to my chest.

We stared at each other for a moment.

"I was suspicious," he said, finally. "Just a weird feeling. Also, you told us you were studying for the GRE, but you don't own a single prep book."

Shit, I thought. I forgot that I had told Katherine that I was planning to go to graduate school, that I wanted to be a child psychologist. It wasn't totally a lie—I didn't *not* want to be a child psychologist—but clearly I hadn't thought it through.

I said nothing.

"You don't look like her," he told me.

"No. I did, a little, when I dyed my hair brown."

"Was that on purpose?"

Why lie? "Yes."

"I guess I can see it. Now that I know."

It was so hot that day. I wanted to be back inside, in the air-conditioning, but I knew neither of us wanted Katherine—or Ruby, for that matter—to hear what we were saying.

"Oh," I said. And then, stupidly, "Are you angry with me?"

He actually laughed at that, but it was not a friendly laugh.

"I'm surprised, and confused. But I don't think 'angry' is what I feel. In a way, it's nice to finally meet you. Sara talked about you a lot."

This made my heart shudder in my chest. "Really?"

"I mean, there wasn't a lot to say, because you were just a baby. She was nervous when you were first born, that your father would forget about her, or something. But she really liked you, thought you were adorable. She showed me a picture of you, at a pumpkin patch. She thought it was the funniest thing in the world."

I knew which photo he was talking about. I was only a year old, very chubby, dressed in an orange jumpsuit. I looked exactly like the pumpkin I was sitting on. My mother had it in a silver frame by her bedside table.

Dizzy, I sat down on the grass, which was still wet from the rain. Blake sat down a few feet away from me. *He is trying not to scare me*, I thought.

"Why are you here, Luna?"

"I want to know the truth," I said. "No one talks about Sara. No one will tell me what I need to know."

"And what is that?"

If I could put it into words, I thought, *I wouldn't be here in the first place.*

"Why did you kill her?"

He sighed. "It wasn't on purpose. You probably already know that. I was out of my mind. I didn't know who I was, what I was doing."

"That's what you told the police. Is it really true?"

"It is. Think about it this way. I admitted it right away. If I wanted to kill her, wouldn't I have tried to get away with it?"

I didn't know what to say to that. We were silent for a long time.

"Do you know who John Logan is?" he asked me.

"The name sounds familiar." I knew a lot about Logan, actually, because I researched him after I read an article about a vigil that was held for his victims as well as for Sara.

"He's a serial killer. Killed six women. The night I spent in jail, he was in the cell next to mine."

"Oh, wow."

"I was pretty out of it at the time, but I remember thinking how dumb he was. Friendly, but stupid, in a very obvious way. I didn't find out what he did until later, and it really shocked me. That someone so stupid could kill six people. Anyway, when my mom found out about this guy, she was like, thrilled. She thought maybe he had killed Sara, not me."

"Did he?"

"No. He was arrested two weeks before Sara went missing. That's a pretty solid alibi."

"Oh."

"I'll admit, I wish it was him. Do you think that's terrible?"

"Kind of."

"I never got to grieve for her. It wasn't allowed. No one wanted to hear about how much I missed her, when I was the one who took her away."

Took her away where? I wanted to ask, but instead I said: "I don't feel sorry for you."

"I don't expect you to. I'm telling you the truth, as per your request. I'm not sure how to make you believe me, because I think you'd rather not. I think it's easier for you to believe that I am the evil man who destroyed your family and got away with it. I did not want to kill Sara. I did not want her to die. I loved her so much. Nothing in my life has ever resembled that kind of love. I was out of my mind. I would not have hurt her otherwise."

I thought his words sounded rehearsed, but I had to consider that he was right, that I didn't want to believe him.

I took a deep breath.

"My father has never been angry with you. At least not as far as I know. I think it's—" I struggled for the right word and eventually settled on "—perverse. He should want you dead. If it was me who was killed, I would want someone to avenge me. And if not my father, then who?"

"No, you wouldn't."

"What?"

"You wouldn't want someone to avenge you if you were killed. You wouldn't want anything, because you'd be dead."

I didn't know what to say to that.

"That's the awful paradox of it. We're all left trying to figure out what the dead person would want, and you can never really figure it out, because they're dead. And even if you did somehow figure it out, you couldn't give it to them."

What would Sara have thought of me being here, speaking to him? I had no way of knowing, of even making an educated guess. Blake knew so much more about her than I ever would. I felt my old fury making my hands ache.

"You moved on," I said. "You got married. You have a job. You have a kid."

"Well, yes. Isn't that what you want me to do?"

"No. I think it's incredibly fucking unfair that you have this whole life and she's just dead."

"Would you have preferred for me to stay in prison for my whole life? Or some mental hospital? Would that help? Don't you want me to be a good husband and father, to give back to my community?"

"I think you're mocking me."

"I most definitely am not. I promise."

I looked at my watch. It was almost eight A.M.

"Ruby will be waking up soon," I said.

"Luna," he answered. "I'm sure you understand, I can't let you stay here."

"Why not?"

"You lied to us. I don't feel safe leaving my kid with you."

"I would never, ever hurt Ruby."

He said nothing. He didn't believe me, I realized. It made me furious. It made me wonder if I was telling the truth.

"That's bizarre," I said. "*You* don't feel safe. At least *I've* never killed anyone.

He said nothing.

"I'm not the crazy one here!" I was yelling now. "It's not crazy for me to want justice for my sister."

"I don't think you're crazy, Luna. And you're not going to believe me when I say this, but I want you to listen anyway. Can you do that?"

"Fine."

"There is no such thing as justice. It's an idea that makes people feel better, that's all. There is only revenge, or mercy. And you can't have both."

We were both silent for a long time. Eventually he stood up and handed me an envelope.

"Here's the money we owe you, and then some. Made out to Luna Morgan."

I was tempted to tear it up in front of him, but instead I shoved it in my back pocket.

"Does Katherine know?"

"No. Not yet."

"Are you going to tell her?"

"I'm not sure how. But yes."

"Please don't," I said. "Tell her something else. That I have mono. That I was stealing her jewelry. Anything."

"Why?"

Because I like her. Because I want to protect her from this sickness. "I just don't want her to know."

He sighed. "We'll see. I don't like lying to her."

We walked toward the house in silence.

"I'll pack up and leave right away," I told him.

"Do you want to say good-bye to Ruby?"

I was surprised to find tears welling in my eyes. "No. I think it's better if I don't."

He watched me as I walked up the stairs. I turned around.

"What do you feel, when you think of Sara now?"

He was silent for a long time, not meeting my eyes. Finally he said: "I miss her. Every single day I think of something I wish I could tell her. A bird I saw, a joke I heard. And if I close my eyes, I can see her face with perfect clarity. But when I try to hear her voice, my heart goes blank."

I went home. I slept through most of August. In September, to my mother's delight, I started studying for the LSAT. I didn't particularly care about going to law school, but I did like the logic problems. I liked how they made it impossible to think of anything else. Six men in six boats. That was all that mattered.

I also started working at the makeup counter of a department store. It was mostly boring, but I was occasionally thrilled by the intimacy of putting makeup on someone else's face. These women, total strangers, allowed me to touch their lips, their eyelids. It was an odd power. My mother stopped by quite often, ostensibly to use my employee discount, but also, I think, because she was worried about me. I didn't tell her or my father why I had left my nanny job so suddenly. I felt bad about leaving it to their imagination, but I didn't know how to explain it to them, either.

One day a co-worker asked me to cover her shift in the children's shoe department, and I agreed. The store was quiet that day. Around noon, a tall, red-haired woman walked in, holding the hand of a little girl. *Katherine*, I thought, and my whole body went cold. What had Blake told her, in the end? Did she hate me? And what had they told Ruby? Did either of them miss me? As the woman approached, I was ready to weep.

"Hi," she said. "We're looking for some party shoes. Can you help us?"

It was not Katherine. Up close, I could see that her hair wasn't even really red, but blonde. The girl holding her hand was closer to three or four. It was not them. It was not them. I felt tears drip down my face.

"Are you OK?" the woman asked, alarmed.

"Yes," I said, wiping my face with my sleeve. "Allergies, I'm sorry." I knelt down so that I was eye level with the little girl. "Now, what are we looking for today?"

Sara

Maggie and Jessica's dad, Robert, gets home a full hour after he said he would. He is divorced and his daughters only spend the weekends with him, so he says he feels bad about leaving them with a babysitter, but he had to go to a work thing. Sara thinks this probably means a date, and the fact that he came home late, and looking dejected, makes her think so even more. She's an expert in the foibles of divorced parents, her own having been separated for almost five years. An amicable divorce, according to them.

Sara's father remarried, a very nice, normal woman named Colleen. They recently had a cute little baby named Luna. Sara expected to resent Luna, but she adores her, even offers to babysit for free. Sara loves babies. They're like dolls and puppies combined. Colleen keeps declining the offer, probably afraid that Sara is secretly jealous and will smother Luna in her crib.

Because he feels bad about being late, Robert gives Sara ten dollars more than he owes her. He also offers to give her a ride home.

"I have my bike," she says.

"We can put it in the trunk. Come on, I don't like you being out alone this late."

Exactly how old does he think she is? Sara is amused. She's been eighteen for two weeks now. Still, she accepts his offer. She's a sucker for old-fashioned male protectiveness, probably because her father is one of those new-age feminist guys who would never threaten to shoot a guy for looking at his daughter the wrong way. This analysis is courtesy of Sara's best friend, Dawn, who considers herself a kind of genius when it comes to daddy issues.

Sara has known Dawn since they were in elementary school. They took ballet classes together. Sara just liked the tutus and the ribbons, but Dawn was into the discipline, the way the dull pain made her mind sharper. They didn't really become friends until tenth grade. At the beginning of high school Dawn was one of the cool girls. Her star fell after a rumor circulated that she had Done It with two guys at the same time. This lowered Dawn to the same rung of the food chain that Sara occupied. First they were lab partners, badly screwing up chemistry experiments together, and then they were friends.

Being a teenage girl is hard, because you have to become sexual at the exact right time, in the exact right way. If you do it wrong, or too early, no one will want you anymore. But if you're too slow, then you'll get left behind, and no one will want you then, either. Sara got it more or less right because of her boyfriend, Jack. Dawn once described him—"like a witch turned a golden retriever into a person." He's very sweet, almost handsome, not that smart. Sara likes him. She even likes having sex with him, but she's glad college will give her an easy way to break up with him.

Robert's car is such a dad car, Sara observes. She wonders if he and his date fucked in the backseat. If they did, he probably wouldn't have looked so sad when he came home. Sara doesn't like the idea of adults having sex the way teenagers do. Either they should fuck in five-star hotels, or they should be as celibate as monks. Otherwise it's just depressing.

She watches Robert as he drives. He is kind of handsome, but mostly generic. He could be an illustration in a textbook for learning English. *Father, dad, daddy, papa.*

"You're going to have to give me directions," he says.

"Oh. Left at Bolton."

He obeys.

"So," he asks her, "what grade are you in?"

"I just graduated, actually."

"Wow. Congratulations."

"Thanks." Sara thinks it's stupid that people keep congratulating her for graduating from high school. It would be one thing if she was the first person in her family to do so, or if she had a disability, or something like that. But Sara went to a private school with less than a hundred kids per grade. *Not* graduating would be remarkable. At the moment, all she's done is meet expectations.

"What's next?"

"Uh, college, I guess. You're going to turn right on Bryant."

"Where?"

"Crawford. So pretty close by."

"Crawford. That's like, art school, right?"

"Pretty much."

She wants to tell him that she got into SAIC, and CalArts as well, but chose Crawford because she didn't want to be too far away from her mother. Why does she want to impress him? Just some suburban dad. What does he know about art, or her, or anything?

"You're going to stay on here for a while, and then it's a right on North Street," she tells him.

"Gotcha."

Sara leans against the window. The cold glass feels good against her forehead.

"So did the girls give you any trouble?"

"No, never. They're angels."

He laughs. "With you, maybe. With me, Jesus, you'd think it was like I'm marching them off to war every time

I try to get them in the car. To do anything, swimming, summer camp, whatever, it's always a fight. God forbid I have to take them to the dentist, because then it's a full-scale rebellion."

Sara laughs. She suspects it's usually Maggie and Jessica's mother who takes them to the dentist.

"Well, they're always well behaved with me," she says.

"You must have magic powers."

"I don't think so! One of the kids I look after, he's seven, and the only way I can get him to brush his teeth and go to bed is to threaten him with his own water gun."

Robert laughs. It is not like Jack's laugh, but coarser, and quieter.

They pull up in front of Sara's house. She really could have taken her bike.

"Thanks for the ride. Give me a call if you need me to look after them again."

He helps her get her bike out of the trunk. As she walks it into her garage and puts it in its place, she can feel him watching her. She could just go inside, but it seems rude not to say good-bye. She walks back to the car.

"Thanks for the ride," she says again.

"Wait," he says. "I'm going to give you an extra ten, for being so flexible about staying late."

"You already—" she starts to say, but he's already sliding the bill into the back pocket of her shorts. His hand stays there for a few seconds, during which Sara becomes unusually aware of her own heartbeat, its rhythm and strength.

Then he squeezes her ass. She turns around, shocked, and he kisses her, hard, but not so forcefully that she can't pull away.

"What the fuck!" she says.

She looks at him, expecting to see embarrassment, or even surprise: *I can't believe I just did that!* But Robert looks angry, as if he wants to hit her. Sara takes a step backward. She's only a few yards from her house. The light in her mother's bedroom is still on. Her neighborhood, always so still and quiet, is suddenly humming with life. She can hear every radio playing, every dishwasher running, every blade of grass murmuring with ants and mosquitos.

Robert gets in his car and drives away. Sara waits until she's inside, with the front door locked, to check if the money is still in her pocket. It is.

Sara's mom is in bed, lying on top of the covers, watching a documentary on TV. She's always watching something on the History Channel or Animal Planet, something educational. It makes Sara sad. Why can't she just watch a soap opera like a normal person? It's like she's trying to improve herself, like she thinks knowing a lot about the Spanish Inquisition or endangered species of sharks will lead to a better life.

"Hi, Mom."

"Hi, angel." Her mother beckons her over and hugs her.

"You smell good," Sara says.

"I took a long bath. Candles and everything."

Which women's magazine told her to do that? Sara squeezes her mother's hand. "I can tell. Your fingers are all pruney."

Her mother laughs and turns the volume on the television down.

"How was babysitting?"

"Fine. They're sweet girls. We watched *Pocahontas*."

"Great. You fed them, cleaned them, all that?"

"Yup."

Sara wonders what would happen if she told her mother about what Robert did. It feels like it happened a week ago, even though it took her less than a minute to walk up the stairs.

How would her mother react? Outrage, definitely. She might even call the police. Or she might call Sara's father and demand that he deal with it, insist that he defend his daughter's honor, some medieval shit like that. Sara knows—she knew the second that it happened—that she's not going to tell her mother, that it would not be worth causing her so much anxiety.

Everyone knows that parents will do anything to protect their children, Sara thinks, holding her mother's lavender-scented hand. No one talks about what children do to protect their parents.

"I'm going to go over to Dawn's," she says.

"Really? It's so late."

"It's a Saturday," Sara reminds her. "And summer."

"That's true. Are you going to sleep over?"

Sara shrugs. "Maybe."

"Is Jack going to be there?"

"Jack's in Hawaii," she reminds her.

"Lucky Jack."

Sara is actually kind of upset that Jack didn't invite her to join his family on their vacation. That's what people *do*, isn't it, especially if they've been dating for more than a year? Either Jack's parents don't like her, which she's always suspected, or he's planning to break up with her, which would be annoying, even though she's probably going to break up with him before she starts college.

She doesn't feel that strongly about it. She can't even really think about Jack for that long without getting distracted by something else, which is probably a sign that they should just end things already.

Tonight the something else distracting her is Robert, his hand on her ass, his boring face. Thinking about it makes her queasy, makes her want to leave the room, like her mother might be able to figure out what's going on just by looking at her.

"Good night," Sara says.

"Good night. Eat something before you go out, OK?"

"I will," Sara lies, leaving her mother there in her cocoon of lavender.

.   .   .

When she arrives at Dawn's house, Sara finds her friend in the middle of a very messy room. There are two suitcases open on the floor, each of them half-filled with unfolded clothes. Dawn is going to Stanford. She doesn't give a shit about leaving anyone behind.

Sara already knew Dawn was starting college a full week before she was. But seeing the suitcases surprises and upsets her. She wants to lock them both in Dawn's room forever, or, failing that, follow her to California. Sara pushes some clothes aside and sits down on the bed.

"What's going on with you?" Dawn asks. She is braiding and unbraiding her long red hair, which she does when she's bored.

"Weird night," Sara says. "You're packing already?"

"Weird how? And 'packing' is a strong word. I'm just deciding what stuff I want to bring."

"That's packing."

"So I'm a little excited. Sue me." She rummages around under her bed and finds a bottle of very cheap rum and hands it to Sara. "Why was your night weird?"

"I babysat these two girls. And then their dad gave me a ride home, because he said it was too late for me to be out alone. And then he grabbed my ass and tried to kiss me." She wants to tell it like a funny story, but it doesn't come out that way.

"What the fuck?" says Dawn.

"I know."

"Unless, like, was it hot? Like, do you have a crush on him or something?"

"No." Sara shakes her head. "Not even a little bit."

"How old is he?"

"I don't know. Dad-aged."

"That's so gross. You should call the police."

"It wasn't that big of a deal. And I am eighteen."

Fair game, that's what eighteen means. Sara takes a long swig out of the bottle.

"If you're too young to ride your bike home at night, you're too young to fuck," Dawn answers firmly.

"He didn't fuck me."

"He would have! Given the opportunity."

"You've never even met him," Sara laughs. Dawn's overprotectiveness is endearing.

"I bet he would have. Sometimes I just want to like, murder every single dude I see."

"That's probably excessive. Maybe we can just, like, blind them. Hot poker to the eyes."

"What about Jack?"

"Jack is probably fucking some girl in a hula skirt as we speak," says Sara. She thinks for a moment. "I'm happy for her, actually."

"What? Happy for who?"

"The hula skirt girl. I mean, Jack is a nice guy. He's gentle. He won't give her shit about wearing a condom. And his dick is big, but not *too* big."

As a point of fact, Jack's dick is the only one Sara has seen in real life, so she can't really comment on its relative size, but that doesn't matter. Dawn has collapsed on a pile of her own clothing, laughing.

"You're a fucking saint, you know that?" she says.

"I know. Saint Sara, Our Lady of Mediocre Boyfriends." Dawn picks up her blow-dryer from her desk.

"Just say the word," she says, brandishing it dramatically. "And I'll kill him for you. I swear I will."

"Jack?"

"No, the creep. The dad."

"Oh."

"Though I'll kill Jack, too, if that's what you want."

Sara shakes her head. "I don't even care. He's just some pathetic guy. Not worth the time and effort."

Dawn takes the rum from her. "You know what? I bet he's at home, right now, jerking off, thinking about you."

"Ew. That does not make me feel better."

"I thought you didn't need to feel better. I thought you didn't care."

Sara giggles. She's a little drunk. "Are you trying to trick me? What's going on here?"

"No! I'm not. I mean, I am, kind of. I'm just saying, it's OK if you do care. It's OK to be mad and grossed-out when someone does something gross. Because that's *why* they do it, you know?" Dawn is bouncing a little, which makes Sara think she started drinking before Sara got there. "Like, it's not because your ass is so gorgeous he can't help himself. Not that your ass isn't gorgeous. But it's because he's some lonely pathetic asshole, and he sees you, and you're young and pretty and smart and about to go to college, and he wants to think he's better than you, but he's not, so he has to grab your ass. Do you see what I'm saying?"

Sara nods. "He gave me ten dollars."

"What?"

Sara is now laughing so hard she has to bite her arm to keep from making too much noise. "Ten dollars! Is that all my ass is worth?"

Dawn is laughing, too. "Unbelievable. What a fucking cheapskate. On top of everything. You know what? I bet he meant to give you, like, a fifty-dollar bill, to make himself feel powerful. But then that was all he had in his wallet."

"He deserves to die for being so cheap. Ten dollars!"

"Do you have it with you?"

She does. She takes it out of her pocket and holds it aloft like a trophy. "What the fuck am I going to do with ten dollars?"

"All the liquor stores are closed already."

"We could go to a movie tomorrow," Sara suggests. This is their favorite activity during the summer. The movie theater is air-conditioned, and it's extremely easy to sneak in alcohol via Coke bottle.

"No, we should do something real tonight. I'm worried if we wait, it will lose its magic."

"What magic? What the fuck are you talking about?" Sara laughs, but she knows exactly what Dawn is talking about. She could never explain it to anyone else on earth, but she knows.

"Let's call Owen," Dawn suggests. "He's probably getting off work around now."

"Sure," says Sara, trying to keep her face straight, but breaking into giggles. Owen is Dawn's cousin. He lived with Dawn's family for a few months when Sara was in tenth grade. She had a huge crush on him. If Dawn knew, she never mentioned it. Of course she knew, Sara realizes.

"Where is he working?"

"The 7-Eleven on Showalter."

"Thrilling."

"I know. They don't have real booze but they definitely have beer."

"Even more thrilling. Can we borrow your mom's car?" Dawn's dad's car is a Maserati. Just being near it makes Sara nervous, like if she looks at it the wrong way it will get a dent and she'll be liable. Once, Dawn's dad picked them up from a school dance in it, and Sara practically held her breath the whole way home. Dawn's mom drives a much less terrifying Volvo.

Dawn considers. "Not worth it. She'll make it into a big thing. She hates Owen."

"She does? He's her nephew."

"Technically my dad's nephew. And he hates him, too. Calls him a reprobate."

Sara shakes her head. Dawn's family fascinates her. They are so good at maintaining the facade of the Best American Family, and Dawn is willing to play along. In return for her performance—good grades, an indispensable member of the cheerleading squad—Dawn's parents never dig too deep in their daughter's life.

They'd probably be horrified by what they found, even if Dawn's escapades are well within the norm of suburban teenage shenanigans. One time, however, she got Sara to help her perform a satanic ritual involving tea lights and lots of chalk, but they both chickened out when they realized the ritual demanded the sacrifice of a small animal. They used one of Sara's old teddy bears instead. That weekend, the cheerleading squad took home a state medal, so, according to Dawn, the ritual worked.

They ride their bikes to the 7-Eleven. The parking lot is empty except for Owen's car, a Ford that looks like it narrowly escaped being turned into scrap metal, and a white van.

"Serial killer," says Dawn, pointing.

Sara checks around the side. "Nope. Dry cleaners." She points to the company's name, written in big blue letters.

"A front, obviously," Dawn answers. She sounds disappointed.

Owen is behind the register, filling out a crossword puzzle. It's such an old-man thing to do, a contrast with his long hair and sleepy eyes. It makes Sara remember, vividly, why she liked him so much. This time, though, she notices the acne on both his cheeks. If her skin was that bad, Sara thinks, she would never be able to leave the house. She hates herself for having such a mean thought and smiles at him brightly as if that makes up for it. He grins back in a lazy, enticing way, and the smile and the eyes cancel out the bad skin. *Is it normal to think like this, like a boy is an equation?* Sara wonders if she drank more than she meant to.

"Hello there," Dawn says, in a funny, elegant accent, like that of an old-movie star. "We'll have two glasses of your finest Mountain Dew."

"Yes, milady." He bows mockingly. *Not medieval*, Sara thinks, *old Hollywood*. No one except her and Dawn ever gets these things right.

Sara and Dawn share a cigarette outside while Owen closes up. The white van is gone.

"Off to go cut off some poor girl's head, no doubt," Sara says. "Though that sounds like a lot of effort. Physically, I mean."

"Ugh, yeah. Strangling is so much easier." But the way Dawn says it, Sara can tell she isn't having fun anymore.

It's interesting, the ways in which Dawn is tough, and the ways she isn't. Grown men yelling obscenities at her on the street, sneering teachers, DAWN=WHORE written in Sharpie in a bathroom stall—these things don't bother her at all. But once, during lunch at school, a girl started to describe a scene from a horror movie, and Dawn got up and left without a word. Sara found her sitting on the edge of the football field, gray-faced, digging her nails into the dirt.

Owen comes out. Dawn allows him the last drag of the cigarette as they walk to the vacant lot a block over. There, under the dull glow of a streetlamp, Owen rolls a joint and Sara and Dawn drink the beers he brought along. They talk easily, quietly, about nothing. Sara and Owen are sitting very close, their thighs almost touching. She can tell he's watching her but doesn't know what he's looking for. If she cheated on Jack, Dawn wouldn't tell, but she'd probably feel bad. Her fourteen-year-old self, with her fourteen-year-old crush, seems so present it's like a fourth person hanging out with them. Midway through the joint, Dawn interrupts.

"Let's go swimming," she says. "I'm in the mood to swim."

"That sounds fun," says Sara, dubiously. "At your house?"

"No, at the club."

Until a few weeks ago, Dawn worked at the country club where her parents are members, teaching tennis to small children at summer camp. Sara has been there twice, once for Jack's sister's wedding, which was fun, and once for Dawn's debutante ball, which was not.

"You still have keys and stuff?"

"They don't use keys. Everything's like, codes that you punch in, and I know those."

"You're crazy," says Owen. "Those places have a million security cameras."

"Not at the pool entrance," says Dawn confidently. Sara doubts she knows this for a fact. "Besides I met the security guards and they truly don't give a shit. They'll see the tapes in the morning, be like, *What the fuck?*, and then just delete them like they usually do. They don't save the footage."

Sara is dying to ask what television show Dawn watched to come up with this, but knows better. When she's in this kind of mood, Dawn hates being interrupted. She'll get hurt and angry, and then the whole night will go to shit.

"I'm in," Sara says.

Owen looks at her, alarmed. "You're crazy. We could go to jail."

Dawn scoffs. "What are they going to do, track me down to California? For swimming?"

"*I'm* not going to California," Owen says. "Neither is Sara, actually. You're so full of shit, Dawn."

"So don't come. We don't need you."

Owen looks at Sara again, as if begging for an ally. She shrugs. It would be nice to have Owen there, but it's not necessary.

"See ya," she says. "Thanks for the beer."

Sara and Dawn hop on their bikes and ride away, leaving Owen there in the dim neon, watching them go.

· · ·

The gates that surround the country club are more impressive and sinister than Sara thought they would be. Each pole narrows to a sharp, elegant tip. It looks like something out of a children's storybook. It makes her want to get inside even more, but she can't help but ask Dawn, "Are you sure you want to do this?"

"One hundred percent," Dawn answers, leaning her bike against a tree. "This is the furthest gate from the main entrance," she explains. "See, no cameras."

It's too dark for Sara to know whether she's right. Anyway, she doesn't care. Some part of her brain might still be worried about getting caught, but her body doesn't. It's limber and fluid and burning. All she wants is to be in the water. Dawn runs her hand along the gate until she finds a metal box and opens it. She punches in six numbers, and then the gate opens with a low, welcoming groan.

"There we go," she says. Sara pretends not to be impressed.

They work together to pull the cover off the pool. "Usually there are like six dudes in boat shoes who do this," Dawn says, breathing heavily.

"Welcome to the revolution," Sara answers, and they both laugh so hard they have to sit down for a moment.

They give up and leave the pool cover half-on, half-off. "Good enough," Dawn proclaims. They take off their clothes and get in the water. Sara expected to keep her bra and underwear on, but Dawn gets completely naked, so she does, too. She imagines some fat security guard in a windowless office somewhere, watching them, and it makes her giddy.

Sara swims a few horizontal laps. She is a good swimmer. She can feel all her muscles and bones moving together perfectly. It feels even better naked. When she comes up for air, she has to pull her wet, heavy hair from in front of her face.

"I feel like a mermaid," she tells Dawn.

"Whatever makes you happy," Dawn answers. She is floating, her arms and legs stretched out as if she were making a snow angel.

"You're bored already, aren't you?" asks Sara.

"No," Dawn snaps, and then, "Yes. A little."

"I knew it!"

"Fuck. What's wrong with me?"

I wish I knew, Sara thinks. "Nothing. You just need some pills, probably. Or a boyfriend."

"Yeah, sure." Dawn flips over and disappears underneath the water for a few seconds. When she reemerges, she says: "It would be nice to meet someone who doesn't immediately make me want to claw my fucking eyes out."

"Like Jack?"

"No offense, but yeah."

"None taken. You'll find someone in college, I bet."

"I hope so."

"Of course you will." Sara gestures to Dawn's body, naked in the darkness. "Look at you. You're stunning."

"You literally can't see me."

"I know what you look like!"

This makes Dawn laugh, and Sara relaxes. She swims more laps, practices handstands and tumble turns. She has no way of knowing how much time is passing.

"Is it starting to get light out?" she asks Dawn.

"I don't think so. I think our eyes are just getting used to the dark. I don't know. Do you want to go home?"

"I'm cold," Sara admits.

They get dressed in their dry, flimsy clothes. They pull the plastic cover back over the pool. They ride their bikes back to Dawn's house. As they approach the driveway, Sara stops abruptly.

"Fuck," she says. "I totally forgot." She pulls the ten-dollar bill out of the pocket of her shorts.

"What?"

"Owen just gave us the beers, so we didn't use my money. My cursed money."

Dawn bursts into laughter.

"What are you going to do with it?"

Sara smooths the bill against her thigh. She holds it up as if inspecting it. Without asking, she takes a lighter from Dawn's purse and sets the bill on fire. She holds on to it for as long as she can, until the flames come too close to her fingers, and then she drops it on the ground.

"Shit," says Dawn finally. She stamps out the flames with her flip-flops. "You're fucking crazy." But Sara knows she is impressed.

Some grass and wildflowers have grown up through the concrete, stubborn as children. Among them, the embers glitter like a hundred hungry eyes.

ACKNOWLEDGMENTS

This book would not exist without the kindness of many people. I am not capable of thanking as deeply as they deserve, but I will try.

My most heartfelt thanks to my agent, Julia Masnik, who believed in this book way before it was actually any good.

And to Paul LaFarge, for introducing us.

To my editor, Callie Garnett, and everyone at Bloomsbury for giving this strange story a good home.

To Rivka Galchen, Elissa Schappell, Lara Vapnyar, Yelena Akhtiorskaya, Darcey Steinke, and all the wonderful, generous people at the Columbia MFA program.

To Susannah Slocum, for her wisdom and insight.

To Michael Hanna, for his kindness and brilliance.

To Nicole Ouzounis, my true ride or die. Thanks for literally helping me not die.

To Rebecca Godfrey, who I am outrageously blessed to have as both a mentor and friend.

To my friends, those beautiful people who graciously let me babble about murder for three years without complaint.

And to my family, for allowing me to become the person I needed to be to write this book.

I love you all so much more than I can say.

READING GROUP GUIDE

1. *'Even if they didn't know her well, their proximity to something so cruel would change their world.'* The novel is narrated by twelve characters, all of whom are in some way connected to the victim. Why do you think the author chose this type of narration? What does it do that a single narrator couldn't?

2. What does the novel have to say about how society tends to treat young women who are victims of violence? How do the characters' memories of Sara contrast with the way her story was portrayed in the media?

3. *'She forgave Blake, but it was irrelevant. She didn't forgive him because he deserved it, but because she loved him, and she probably only loved him because he was handsome and kind to her'.* How does the novel approach the question of forgiveness? Do you think Katherine's decision to forgive Blake is justified?

4. Discuss the role of humour in the novel. Which parts made you laugh? What makes humour a useful tool for processing such a difficult topic?

5. Why do you think the author chose to focus not on the victim, but on the people left behind? Can you think of any other novels, films or TV shows that give these people a voice?

6. *'What I felt when I saw that frozen face was not fear or disgust. It was relief. It lasted only a moment, but it was so profound that it bordered on joy.'* Discuss the author's treatment of complex emotional reactions. Why do you think Marianne felt something close to joy when she discovered the body?

7. What makes Jessica curious to begin her correspondence with the prisoner? What do you imagine he says to her in his responses? How does it make you feel to realise that the letters are a source of companionship for her?

8. *'He could have sworn it was her. The woman sitting next to him on the plane looked so much like Sara ... The illusion lasted only a second, but it rattled him.'* In what ways are the characters haunted by Sara? Why do you think the author shows us fleeting moments like this one?

9. When we meet Blake later on in the novel, he is living happily with his wife and child. How does this make you feel? How do you think Blake feels? Did you expect a greater sense of resolution at the end of the novel?

10. Reviewers have praised *Nothing Can Hurt You* for playing with and subverting the tropes of the 'dead girl' genre. Do you agree with this? How does the novel achieve this?